Phoebe

Phoebe

Design and production by Daniela K. Robins, Robins Wings Publishing Company

First Edition

1 2 3 4 5 6 7 8 9 10

ISBN-13: 978-1-950814-35-0

Library of Congress Control Number: 2022950838

Robins Wings Publishing Company

Chesapeake, VA

Phoebe

by

EUNICE HUBERTA TOBIE

WITH CONTRIBUTIONS FROM
DANIELA K. ROBINS
DENNIS R. RIDLEY, PH.D.

ROBINS WINGS PUBLISHING COMPANY
CHESAPEAKE, VA

Foreword

After publishing my grandmother's book, *Belle*, written by Naomi Tobie Ridley about her grandmother, Belle Reed Miller Fletcher, my Papa and I were very interested to learn from my Uncle Art that my great-grandmother, Eunice Huberta Tobie, was quite the writer too. She wrote this book, *Phoebe*, about many of the same ancestors of mine that appeared in *Belle*. One difference was that Eunice used pseudonyms for many of their names. Eunice writes her own story as a participant, including her family entering the story at various points. Therefore, we thought it would be helpful to give the cast of characters and who they were in real life, which we show on the next page.

Daniela K. Robins

Cast of Characters

Cast Name	Actual Name
Phoebe	Eunice Huberta Miller
Tom	Harvey Elmer Tobie
Mama	Sarah Belle (Reed) Miller/Fletcher
Papa	Silas Metcalf Fletcher
Helen	Rita Belle (Fletcher) Abbott
William	Silas Milton Fletcher
"Beloved Aunt"	Gracie May (Reed) Libby/Thurston
Maria Reed	Laura Maria (Farwell) Reed
Grandfather Reed	George M. Reed
Uncle Will	Will Doak Reed
Sammy Reed	Richard M. Reed
Aunt Etta	Etta Lucinda Reed
Uncle Hiram	Hiram Farwell
Uncle Dick	Richard Farwell
Ed	Edward Farwell
Hubert Miller	Hubert M. Miller
Mrs. Goodlow	Nancy (Farlow) Miller
Little Maria	Gertrude (Gertie) Miller
Uncle Archie	Archie Clifford Libby
Rocky	Rocky Orestas Conser
"Helen"	"Helen of Troy"
Dr. Moors Farwell	Dr. Moors Farwell
James McAlpin	James McAlpin

Chapter 1 - Letters

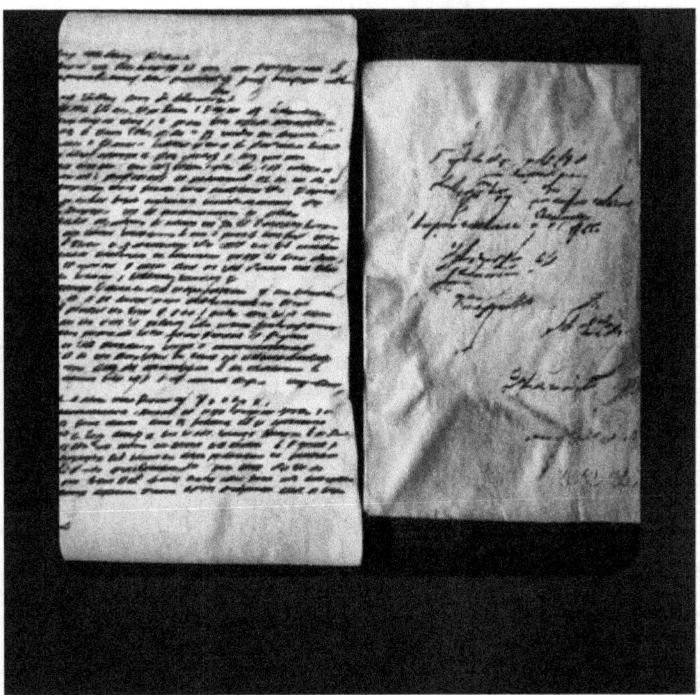

Phoebe

Phoebe sat, poised, finishing the second long letter she had written this sunny March Monday. Quite a chore, these family letters, reflected Phoebe. Here I am, forty-seven years old, going on forty-eight, battling away at my problems as energetically and even as hopefully as I began. And my mother has been doing this twenty-two years longer than I have. Twenty-two years! Mother is almost seventy. Poor Mother. Talk about battles. What a gallant fight she has put up. Left a widow at twenty-two with one baby girl a year old and another baby girl to be born in a month, a tiny seven-month babe. That was I.

And here I am, forty-seven, going on forty-eight, with a married daughter, a college graduate with her Phi Beta Kappa pin; an in-between daughter who has gone back to college for spring term, and that lanky freshman son also gone back for the spring term. And then there's Tom, thought Phoebe, with a tenderness stealing around her lips. Oh, God, let there always be Tom! Let the children come and go, if must be, let them even stay away, but let there always be Tom coming home to me from work at night. Tom, with his unruffled patience, his unfailing fairness, his need of me, his maddening obstinancy, his more than human charity for human frailty. Ah, Tom! Phoebe sighed and dipped her pen down to the paper for the closing paragraph.

"About Mama, William, let's try not to worry too much about her, but this loss of memory is a little frightening, even a temporary loss. You have lived with her all these years, and no one knows better than I how good you have been and are to her. I'm sure Helen will agree. Yesterday I sensed your worry, but there was no chance to talk to you alone. I've written to Helen, so she will not be altogether unprepared should there be a repetition of this recent incident. It seems to me that we (Helen, you, and I) must somehow see to it that Mama has a change, and a lessening of work, worry, and responsibility. Do you suppose a month with me would help? Clarice's room will be vacant until June, and it is warm, has a good bed, and is next to the bathroom.

"Try to get Mama to visit me for a month, William. You are the only one who can persuade her because she so firmly believes that you can't do without her! Of course, I know that is nonsense. And so does Helen. But Mama believes it, and so it is so as far as she is concerned. Mama has always tried to do more than she is able to do. Even at almost seventy, she hasn't learned to rest but must go into every detail of her tasks with the same minute devotion she gave to her children's upbringing. And she just can't stand the strain, William. She has overtaxed herself again over getting one set of renters out of her house and another set into it. She has worked too hard, walked too far, and attempted too much. She burns up every scrap of energy she has, then ventures far beyond the bounds of safety and judgment because there is still something left undone! What an adorable, annoying woman she is!

"Tell her I am lonely, William, and she owes her eldest a little consideration. Maybe she will come, after all, and we can coax her into a more restful frame of mind. Yes, I believe she has suffered an attack of amnesia. It was a temporary escape for her, and it is just as well that she makes light of it. But it oughtn't to happen again. It might be a stroke next time, and Mama would rather be dead than helpless. She mustn't get chilled or overtired again. And she mustn't get up so early mornings or climb up on chairs. She has those dreadful dizzy spells and is simply inviting disaster from a fall. Shall we hire a woman to come twice a week and do the heavy work? Oh yes, I know Mama will be furious, but perhaps she will get used to it and will finally give in. Let's try it, William.

Lovingly,

Phoebe"

Chapter 2 - Moors Farwell

Phoebe

Phoebe's great-grandfather on her mother's side had been a doctor. Phoebe recalled certain quaint stories of Dr. Moors Farwell that her mother told: stories of a very forthright man who lived uprightly and dealt justly, although somewhat whimsically at times, with the frailties of his patients. During her little girlhood, Phoebe once spent a summer with a beloved aunt, a sister of her mother's. It was this summer that Phoebe stumbled upon some information concerning this great-grandfather Farwell. In a bureau drawer, she found a document, worn entirely through at folds, which, put together with patient fingers, yielded the following:

Obituary

On the 12 of November 1854, in the 73rd year of his age, Dr. Moors Farwell departed this life at his residence in Mercer County, Illinois. In his decease, his children have lost a good father, the community a good citizen, and the church a useful member. But although he is called from a world of labor to one of glory, his work of benevolence has not ceased, for his life of faith and good works is known and read by all men, and by this, he being dead yet speaketh. The writer offered the consolation of the gospel to his family and neighbors on Sunday, December 31st, in a funeral sermon in his old mansion from Philippians 1:21: "For to me, to live is Christ and to die is gain."

Dr. Moors Farwell was born in New Ipswich, New Hampshire October 13, 1782, but was chiefly reared at Harvard, Massachusetts, where he received a liberal education and studied medicine. He was married to Miss Sarah Jewett at Bolton, Massachsetts, after which he returned to his native place, where he remained pursuing his profession until the summer of 1841 when he moved to this place.

Chapter 2

Here his companion died on Sept. 4, 1849, leaving him with a large family of mostly grown-up sons and daughters. Being of a feeble constitution and his occupation a very laborious one, he fell into an early decay so that he could not be out much for the last three years of his life. But he passed the time in comparative comfort in the competency of this world's goods and the fruit of industry and economy. Father Farwell was trained in Calvinistic theology by good and pious parents, but he found the doctrine too cruel for his broad and benevolent soul. At an early age, he embraced the benevolent and uncomplicated faith of a believer in the basic elements of Christianity —salvation from sin and death through our Lord Jesus Christ. "For it is by grace you have been saved, through faith—and this is not from yourselves, it is the gift of God—not by works, so that no one can boast." Ephesians 2:8-9. A belief he proved to be good to live by and still better to die by. May his children and friends looking to his good example learn to practice his virtues, and if he had any faults, as all mortals have, learn to shun them that they may live the life of the righteous and their last end be like his.

Sweet is the scene when virtue dies!
When sinks a righteous soul to rest,
How mildly beam the closing eyes,
How gently heaves the expiring breast!

W. E. Reilly

Preemption, Illinois, Jan. 1st, 1855

Phoebe felt strangely excited over her discovery. From her aunt, she extracted every particle of information possible about this doctor ancestor. Around him, she wove a setting, a foundation for her own life and philosophy. Here was a man she felt she knew, one whom she longed to know better. Somehow, peculiarly, he seemed to belong to her more than anyone she knew in the flesh. In one thing, she failed; to find out where his father figured in the American Revolution. Phoebe's mother couldn't tell.

"It's all so long ago, child, and the family has lived in the west so long. What difference does it make?" What difference! Phoebe was aghast.

"But, Great-grandfather Farwell's father may have been a Tory who supported the British!"

"And what if he were?" asked Mama.

"He must have been a patriot," worried Phoebe, "and yet!" But she gloried in Dr. Moors nevertheless. He was a kindred soul. Phoebe had her agonies over theology. Was she going to be saved? And if she were not, could she do anything to avert her damnation? Out of this dilemma, she had come triumphant. If that was the way God did things, Phoebe would have none of Him! But then she had found Great-grandfather Farwell. Dr. Farwell did not believe in a doctrine so "cruel." She, Phoebe, would embrace a "broad and benevolent faith," too, believing in salvation through the grace of Jesus. She loved the lines that went "and if he had any faults as all mortals have." Phoebe was secretly and immensely pleased over her great-grandfather's faults. She felt sure they were human and lovable faults, traits she wouldn't have missed in him for the world.

Great-grandfather Farwell's Bible was kept in the same bureau drawer. The pages for records were full of painstaking entries. Phoebe poured over these records until she knew from memory the names of these shadowy sons and daughters of Dr. Moors, beginning with Sarah Parker Farwell born September 3, 1811, and died March 3, 1889, and ending with Caroline Farwell born May 28, 1831, and died October 5,

1869. Down the list appeared Maria Farwell, born March 21, 1828, and died March 21, 1889. That was Grandmother Reed, Mama's mother. Phoebe had never seen her; she died on her 61st birthday, two years before Phoebe was born. Mama's mother had been a wonderful woman. All her surviving children agreed with this opinion, particularly Phoebe's Uncle Will, forever a bachelor. Uncle Will always looked so tender when he spoke of his mother.

"You are a good mother," he said more than once to his niece, Phoebe, "but even you are not as good a mother as my mother was." And then he would speak glowingly of the fantastic, proud woman, mother of 12 children. Phoebe was never surprised that Grandmother Maria Reed was a wonderful woman. After all, wasn't she Dr. Moor's daughter? When Phoebe first realized that out of this alarming number of children, Grandmother Maria Reed had raised only four, she went to Mama about it.

"What happened to all of them?" she demanded, "how could eight children in one family die?"

Mama explained about the twins and another infant who scarcely lived at all, about the three children fatally stricken with the dreaded "black measles," a fifteen-year-old sister who died caring for them, and the fourteen-year-old brother who accidentally shot himself while rabbit hunting. Phoebe's eyes grew enormous over this story; she couldn't forget it. Sometimes at night, she woke in terror after repeatedly dreaming the story.

Mama had said, "Sammy must have tried to poke the rabbit from the hedge with the wrong end of his gun, Phoebe, and somehow the gun went off and shot him. Then he started home, but he was bleeding so much, he took just thirteen steps before he fell, and so they found him dead."

"How do you know he took only thirteen steps?" demanded Phoebe feeling horror rising within her.

"There was snow on the ground, and every footprint showed."

Phoebe wondered if Sammy wanted dreadfully to get home. She knew how she would have struggled against pain and loss of blood to get back home to Mama.

Oh, why didn't God help Sammy to hold out until he got home? Maybe that would have been even harder for Maria to bear. Phoebe sobbed terribly into her pillow that night, and Mama was up a long time treating the bad headache that resulted from this welter of emotion.

Chapter 3 – Grandfather Reed

Grandmother Reed's marriage to Grandfather Reed was a love match. The four surviving children spoke tolerantly of George Reed. He had been a good father, a lousy manager, generous, and careless. Born in the South, he was early orphaned, adopted by a young girl in whose family he was being cared for, and kept by her long after her marriage and move to a northern state.

Moving west to Illinois as a handsome young adventurer, he met Maria Farwell, a tiny dark-eyed, vivacious girl. They loved each other, married, and settled down in Mercer County.

But Grandfather couldn't stay settled. The bright hue of gold and the love of adventure drew him like a magnet to California; almost overnight, he joined the overland rush. No one was more daring, more adventurous, more fired with confidence that he would make a fortune in the gold fields. Incredibly, he did.

At first, fortune and all the kindly fates watched over Grandfather. His claim paid amazingly, and he worked furiously to accumulate his stake and get back to the family. After two years of Herculean effort, Grandfather was ready to return. This time it seemed best to go home by ship, and Grandfather was wild with impatience during the tedious journey around the Horn and back to New York. And then the blow fell—while Grandfather slept in a New York hotel, somebody quietly stole his gold dust from under his pillow. His heartbroken efforts to trace his loss were utterly fruitless.

When he arrived home defeated, Grandmother was calm. Perhaps, reflected Phoebe, she liked Grandfather better without the fortune. She presented him with a 16-month-old son he had never seen, and Grandfather returned to farming.

But all the while Grandfather farmed in Illinois, he remembered the West. California—and Oregon—to Grandfather, they meant change. After several years of indifferent crops, tragic thinning in the family ranks, and the death of Sammy, even little Grandmother Maria was ready to journey westward, and Grandfather was eager to transport them. Phoebe's mother barely remembered that trek to California with the four surviving children. Uncle Will was a lad of twelve, his mother's stay, even now more dependable and steady than Grandfather. Mama was six, and Auntie Grace and Aunt Ettie little girls of four and two. Misfortune was not left behind. California was different; Grandfather returned too late for gold, and farming was the only thing left; a dreary prospect to him. The climate was different, money was scarce, and the baby fell sick. She developed infantile paralysis, and they despaired over whether she would live. One day in desperation, Grandmother took her to a Chinese doctor, the only help in sight.

He massaged the paralyzed side and leg with strange ointments and muttered words she did not understand, and Grandmother was afraid to go back. Finally, the ability to walk came back, but the little foot dragged, misshapen and feeble. Aunt Ettie grew up in a world of her own—timid, self-conscious, and fiercely proud. She was tiny, too, and Phoebe's favorite auntie. After Mama and Auntie Grace were each married and moved out, and Grandmother died, Aunt Ettie kept house for Grandfather and Uncle Will. Phoebe's earliest and dearest recollections were bound up with these three lives.

In the meantime, other relatives were moving to Oregon, and one day Grandmother took a stand. She wanted to go to Oregon to live near her people, and she could be firm. This time she was more than usually firm, unnecessarily so, perhaps, because Grandfather was more than ready to go. He was not long converting their few possessions into cash, disposing of the farm, and loading his family on a Portland-bound boat. Phoebe was never tired of listening to Mama's story of this trip by ocean from San Francisco to Portland. Grandfather and Auntie

Grace enjoyed every minute; the others were deathly seasick. At Portland, Uncle Hiram met them. He was a brother of Grandmother's who had settled recently in the Willamette Valley. He had rented a farm for the wanderers, and soon they were settled. Grandmother loved the new home; she blossomed like a rose as her roots went down in the lush soil. Now the children could go to school, and things would get better. They would have a farm, a good one, and money would come, which would mean medical attention for Aunt Ettie.

She reckoned this occurred without Grandfather. No change of scene, climate, or circumstances changed Grandfather; he was a beloved vagabond to the day of his death.

Chapter 4 - New Start

Grandmother struggled to get ahead, and Will worked savagely, beyond his boyish strength, to wrest from the farm all he knew Grandmother longed for in her dreams. Mama learned to keep house, to cook, to raise chickens and turkeys; she found her determination with Grandmother's and Uncle Will's to make a go of things. Auntie Grace helped, too, but Grace never felt the necessity so strongly as the others. She was more like Grandfather; she loved to read, enjoy leisure for its own merits, philosophize and watch the world go by her.

Harvests were good, but prices were low. The family succumbed to ague and fever, and Grandmother suffered from asthma. The brightness of the dream grew a little tarnished, it is true, but the new land held them, even Grandfather. They had never seen such country, such natural loveliness, such return of growth for the effort involved. Uncle Will took over the gardening. Not even the old timers could raise finer vegetables.

Part of the farm was rich river bottom land, sub-irrigated and naturally productive. The family never grew rich, nor yet prosperous, but so long as Grandfather had a penny, they lived on the fat of the land. They were reasonably content, and they were among their own people.

The children had several years of pioneer "schooling," and even Aunt Ettie, vigorously brave, trudged away with the rest to the country school for several months each year. She had a little crutch now and got along nimbly despite the dragging foot, but any mention of her misfortune, any glance at the foot, wounded her to the heart. Phoebe learned early to avoid any reference or glance in that direction, and as long as she lived and as intimately as she loved and knew Aunt Ettie, Phoebe never saw that foot without its stocking and shoe.

These growing young people had fun. Phoebe often teased Mama for details of these good times. They seemed glorious to little Phoebe, who always believed that things beyond her grasp were infinitely more desirable.

One story especially delighted Phoebe: the four young Reeds were visiting overnight with cousins, children of Uncle Dick Farwell. Uncle Dick was, of course, another of Dr. Moors' numerous progeny.

During the early evening, other young people dropped in until the "sitting room" of Uncle Dick's house was lively with boys and girls. Uncle Will and his cousin Ed had retired to an adjacent bedroom to change into more presentable clothes. At the moment when Uncle Will stood clad in his drawers trouser-less, buttoning himself into a clean shirt, Ed treacherously pushed him through the door into the sitting room. He stood in his bare shanks, frantically pounding at a door firmly held on the other side.

Another time Mama, swinging under the big oak, urged Uncle Will to push her higher and higher. He exerted himself to the utmost, and Mama shot high into the oak branches. A giddiness overcame her, and down she fell, striking her chin against the swing board as she dropped. The wound healed into a perfect dimple, much admired by Phoebe.

But the best story of all, thought Phoebe, was the cabbage story. Grandfather had grown some fine cabbages that year and was justly proud of their crisp green heads. One day as he walked through the garden, he discovered a tragedy: all the cabbages were burst open, ruined. Grandfather rushed to the house to ask if anyone knew what had happened to the cabbages. Probably because he was not a stern father, Auntie Grace and Aunt Ettie explained that they had found that sticking a knife into a firm cabbage produced an exciting pop and that they had each procured a knife and enjoyed popping cabbages until there were no more cabbages to explode.

Well, grandfather almost exploded! He picked up a small switch and opined that such naughty girls must be punished, an unheard-of proceeding. Mama couldn't bear it. She began screaming and clutching at her pinafore. "Oh, my heart, my heart!" yelled Mama, working the screams up to an amazing pitch.

Down went the switch while Grandfather, thoroughly taken in, carried Mama into the house. He forgot the cabbages. That was what Mama wanted him to do. Phoebe thought Mama was clever to think of having a heart spell. Secretly, she always intended to have a heart spell of her own someday, at some opportune moment, but the moment for Phoebe never arrived.

Chapter 5 - Hubert and Maria

Mama and Auntie Grace learned to dance, too, and as they grew into slender and pretty girlhood, they had their share of beaux to escort them.

Because of the lame foot, Aunt Ettie couldn't dance. She had fun in other ways. There wasn't any reason why Uncle Will couldn't have danced, except the sufficient one that he didn't care to dance. Uncle Will liked the girls, but he was always afraid of them and imagined himself awkward and tongue-tied in their presence. Perhaps, too, he never found a girl to measure up to Grandmother whom he worshipped. When Phoebe had grown to be quite a big girl of ten years, she found out from Uncle Will that Mama had been the most popular and the prettiest girl in the neighborhood. Mama would never have told her such a thing, Phoebe knew.

But she believed Uncle Will: she looked again at the picture of Mama with her hair shingled and sighed rapturously. Why wouldn't Mama let her, Phoebe, have short hair? Mama looked lovely in the picture. Her eyes were so soft and dark, and the dimple in her chin made her look good enough to eat.

But Mama abhorred the picture.

"Of course, I had to be like all the other silly girls," said Mama, "It isn't a becoming or modest style for young girls." Phoebe could see with her own eyes that it was becoming, and she didn't worry about the modest part.

Mama must have been eighteen when she met Phoebe's father, and he was only a few months older. Hubert Miller was the oldest son of a large family of boys and girls. His mother was a Goodlow. The Goodlows had been neighbors to the Farwells in Illinois and had moved west somewhat earlier.

Phoebe cherished a little anecdote about her two grandmothers. Maria Farwell was a few months older than Maria Goodlow. When the

Goodlows came to the Farwell home to see the new baby, both baby and name were so attractive to Mrs. Goodlow that she asked permission to name her baby, in the event of its being a girl, after the little Maria.

She was a girl and was duly named Maria. So one of Phoebe's grandmothers was named after the other grandmother.

"Of course," reflected Phoebe, "they didn't know they were going to be my grandmothers."

In the Miller family, the scourge of tuberculosis had struck, and Hubert was coughing a little when Mama first became aware of him. After a few months, Mama fell deeply in love with this blue-eyed, shy young man, and they approached Grandmother with their desire to be married. Grandmother had seen much of sickness—Death and she had kept a rendezvous. She sympathized with young love while simultaneously speaking her uncompromising mind; Belle and Hubert were not to be married until he was well. So far as Phoebe ever knew, Mama and Papa did not presume to question this wise ultimatum. Papa saw a doctor and was summarily dispatched for a year of rest in Arizona. Mama was desperately lonely, and Papa was sure he would die, especially now that he and Mama could not even see each other for a whole year.

In the meantime, Mama was soon occupied with a matter that crowded even frustrated love from her heart and mind. Grandmother's frail body became frailer; her jubilant and gallant heart did its utmost to keep beating for these her beloved. How could she leave her improvident, generous husband, her one remaining son, and her three girls? On her sixty-first birthday, the slender thread of her life snapped.

After she had been put away in the little neighborhood cemetery, the family tried to carry on. They all, even Grandfather, tried so pitifully hard. Mama and Uncle Will worked feverishly at farm tasks; Auntie Grace and Aunt Ettie, feeling loneliness almost unbearable, put their shoulders to the family wheel. After a time of great effort, the wheel began to roll, and everyday living was resumed. Young hearts cannot endure too lasting a grief.

Grandfather said little. Increasing deafness was leaving him more and more in a silent world of his own. He read his paper, aired his views on pioneer politics, and lent a hand benignly when he saw something to do. But mainly he smoked his pipe and dreamed by the fire.

And then, almost before even Mama realized, Hubert Miller was back. He looked splendid, his cough was gone, and the doctor said he was well; he wanted Mama to marry him immediately. When Mama told Grandfather the plans for the early wedding, he looked at her mildly, took his pipe from his mouth, and said, "Well, Belle, it's no more than I've been expecting," and he returned the pipe to mouth, and went back to his newspaper.

For a few weeks, the farmhouse hummed with preparations. Grace and Ettie joined forces to make Mama's new clothes. They were married quietly one day at the parsonage and set up housekeeping in a nearby town where Papa had bought and restocked a small hardware store. Papa was determined to keep this new-found health and would not risk farm labor.

Chapter 6 – Tiny Maria

Within the year, folks came over to visit tiny Maria, Mama's and Papa's baby. She was tiny and fair, her skin was petal-like and almost transparent, and her downy hair was already curling in golden loveliness. Mama's and Papa's love for this mite was out of all proportion to her size, probably because behind this fierce love was so much fear.

For the little Maria didn't thrive as a baby should. Her blue eyes were too wide open and wise, and the slightest sounds frightened her. She cried a good deal, and Papa and Mama grew taut-nerved with night vigils. The old doctor, summoned after a particularly bad night, looked her over with frowning intentness.

"Tell me, Doctor," demanded Mama, "does she have consumption?"

"No," said the kind old man, "but she isn't a strong baby. Keep her quiet, let nothing frighten her, and above all," he looked hard at Mama, "be calm yourself." And then he drove away.

Mama needed to keep herself in hand, for a tide of adversity was to bear her fast and far. Papa started coughing again. Another baby was on the way. Luckily, Mama was strong and well and need give no thought to the new life she bore. Hubert Miller's defenses went down with appalling swiftness. They sold the store, and the little family moved in with Papa's family so that he might rest. Doctors, medicine, a hemorrhage, a spell of relief when hope came back, then more dreadful hemorrhages. A month before the premature Phoebe was born, the family buried Papa.

Phoebe never could get Mama to say much of those months with Papa's family, but she wondered mightily about them. For a long time, she only knew that Mama had written to Uncle Will when she— Phoebe, was four weeks old, and Uncle Will had come at once with the farm team and wagon and had moved Mama and her two babies back to her people.

Chapter 6

That was Phoebe's home henceforth. All her life, she had joyous memories of that dear and safe home, with Grandfather, Uncle Will and Aunt Ettie, and Mama and tiny Maria.

Auntie Grace had just been married and moved with her husband to their own home, but Phoebe remembered her almost as well as the others, for Grace and her husband, Uncle Archie, were frequent visitors at the Reed farm.

Grandfather was tenderly proud of these first grandchildren. Maria continued, delicate and shy, terrified if Mama would leave her for an instant. Phoebe was made of sterner stuff. She had survived premature birth and a four-pound start in life. She had survived Mama's getting up after three days and trying to help with the work in the Miller home. Now she successfully survived colic and fretting. She learned early to tuck her tiny hand into Grandfather's and lead him where she wanted him to go. Mama was too busy, tiny Maria was too frail, but Grandfather could and would pay attention to her. He had taken a great deal of care of her from the first, cuddling her in his arms before the fire while he smoked his pipe and read his paper.

One day Mama heard a frightful shriek and found Phoebe writhing. Grandpa, very deaf indeed by this time, was unaware that his pipe had turned over, and it spilled its hot contents onto Phoebe's neck. Phoebe's wound soon healed, but Grandfather couldn't forgive himself for hurting the baby. He became more than ever her champion, her companion, and her comforter. They learned to communicate almost without words. If Grandpa's ears were useless, his eyes were piercingly keen, and his fingers were sensitive. He responded untiringly to the tugs of Phoebe's tiny hands. He plucked thorns from her fingers and feet, he cradled her in his strong arms from the stresses of her little world, and his sympathy healed her pesky wounds. When he drove home from his relatively frequent trips to "town," his pockets always held treats for Maria and Phoebe.

Phoebe had an astonishing memory of events that reached back into her very young childhood. These memories were isolated, not related to the everyday trend of affairs on the farm. One picture held in its scope a portion of a sun-flecked barnyard beneath the giant oaks that grew there. The picture contained Grandpa, Uncle Will, Maria, and Phoebe. A great activity fascinating to Maria and Phoebe was going on. The binder draperies were stretched upon the ground, and Uncle Will, armed with a pair of big shears and a giant curved needle, was sewing patches on worn spots in the draperies. After a bit, Phoebe and Maria began running joyously back and forth across this fascinating carpet. Fun for two little girls, but very naughty and annoying. The picture faded with Mama summarily leading her daughters into the house.

Another picture framed Phoebe and Maria standing before the squat cook stove in the big kitchen. Each child held in her hand a small switch, which she had thrust into the glowing coals behind the grate. When Maria's switch flamed at its tip, she turned to display it to Phoebe and accidentally struck her on the left temple. The hot ash clung to her face, and Phoebe screamed with pain. Into the picture came Auntie Grace, who plucked the torturing coal away. Mama caught her up in comforting arms. Poor little Maria's contrite sobs rang in her ears and mingled with her weeping.

In Mama's red plush album were two pictures of Maria and Phoebe. They are still there after forty-five years. Phoebe often brooded over these pictures as she grew up, having strange thoughts of these sisters. Maria was so lovely: even in the "baby" picture, her wide blue eyes, her golden hair, and her delicacy were Phoebe's envy and delight. In her own dark-eyed, tense face, she saw no beauty, and all her life, Phoebe worshipped beauty and sought to clutch it to herself. She would sit in the corner of the old sofa, Mama's album heavy across her knees, looking hard at the pictures. "Maria is beautiful; I love everything about her." Then she would slide off the sofa, shove a chair against Mama's chest of drawers, climb up, and perch herself before the big mirror, gazing mournfully at her pictured visage. She didn't like herself at all. Brown eyes, red cheeks, dark hair, that round chin. She was a little mollified when Mama made her the beautiful red serge dress with the red velvet yoke and the deep velvet cuffs. There was another picture of Phoebe all alone in that dress. Her hair was cut in bangs, and the bangs were curled and fluffed above her brown eyes. Her little black square-toed shoes were gleaming. It wasn't too bad, but it didn't compare to Maria's blue eyes.

When Maria was four years old, she fell desperately ill. The old doctor's patient horse was hitched to the shiny buggy and stood for long hours tied before the front gate. Phoebe sat on a low stool placed on a corner of the hearth near the old sofa. She faced the closed bedroom door behind which were Mama, the doctor, and Maria. With all her will, she sought to hold back Death. Phoebe didn't know what the abstract concept of death was; she knew very well indeed that something hovered and threatened, and she pushed hard against that dark power. When Mama came weeping through the door one day, Phoebe ran across the floor and laid her cheek against Mama's hand. Mama could not break through her inhibitions long enough to derive comfort from Phoebe's proffer of sympathy.

"Run away, Phoebe, and play." Phoebe returned to her stool, and the dark power rushed over her and carried with it the waning life in the bedroom. Phoebe caught phrases as the family rallied around Mama—spinal meningitis, a word with black and whirring wings; funeral—a dark rite through which they all must pass. Later, Mama led her into the bedroom and lifted her to look at Maria. Then all the dark fears were dissolved—Death was, after all, only a lovely sleep. Maria was more beautiful than ever in her white embroidered dress, her golden curls shining on the white pillow. Phoebe smiled. She thought Mama's tears were very foolish.

The funeral didn't frighten her. She thought the white casket was the most beautiful bed in the world. At the graveside Grandpa took her hand and led her away to look for wild strawberries.

Chapter 7 – Moving forward

Phoebe

Life on the farm must have run rather an uneventful course for the next year or so. Everyone was working hard. Mama took over the care of the chickens and the butter making. Aunt Ettie did the cooking. Uncle Will ran the farm almost single-handedly, with occasional help from Grandpa.

Mama was an attractive young widow, who found herself singled out by more than one marrying-minded single farmer. But Mama was determined to win some peace and forgetfulness for herself. Her detachment and indifference were effectively discouraging.

Phoebe learned to be resourceful in providing entertainment for herself. She devoted herself to a growing family of dolls and set herself the task of dressing and undressing them meticulously. Uncle Will arrived home from town one Saturday evening with a doll carriage which was made to hold all the family on excursions around the house, under the cherry tree, and occasionally across the barnyard to the edge of the woods. Here Phoebe always turned back because the shadows under the oaks were black and mysterious. Someday, Phoebe promised herself sturdily, she would push the doll carriage straight down the road through the shadows with never a glance back to the old farmhouse in the clearing.

In the meantime, she felt the necessity of living in the sunshine and keeping close to her family members. When Mama decided to help run the cook wagon one harvest season, Phoebe had no thought of being left behind. She felt her world shattered when Mama left her with Aunt Ettie and the others. It seemed to Phoebe treachery she couldn't forgive. Mama ought to want her; Mama belonged to her. After several weeks, Mama returned and found a strange Phoebe who stood across the room and refused to come closer to this pretty, radiant woman who coaxed with outstretched arms and growing perplexity on her face. It wasn't naughtiness with Phoebe; it was a wild building up of

35

defenses against another such bereavement. It would be easier, Phoebe thought, not to possess Mama at all than to be torn from her again with no warning.

Years later, Phoebe's almost-grown daughter declared, "Mother always expects the worst." That remark was a knife in Phoebe's heart; she made no answer. She could feel that little Phoebe's choice of the hard way again. Better expect the worst than have it descend unbearably upon you. A strange philosophy, perhaps, to many like her older daughter (Naomi Esther Tobie Ridley), but not so to the Phoebes of the world.

On her fourth birthday, a beautiful thing happened to Phoebe. She and Grandpa had gone with a shiny tin pail searching for wild strawberries in the pasture beyond the oak woods. With Grandpa holding her hand, the shadows held no terrors, only excellent green plants beneath the oak shrubs and lovely green grass on either side of the hard path. But the strawberries, like Phoebe, loved the sun and shone like rubies in the short grass of the meadow.

Grandpa was seventy-six that summer and just a bit breathless when he stooped over too quickly. Phoebe chased butterflies and popped many red berries into her mouth, but she worked, too, for Phoebe felt her responsibilities. Something made her try to do her share; if she evaded, she always felt so ashamed, and she hated herself when she had to be ashamed.

When Phoebe's shadow had grown twice as long as Phoebe and the shiny pail was full, she and Grandpa returned home. And here, waiting, was the lovely surprise: a neighbor's 16-year-old daughter had brought Phoebe a big doll, a glorious doll with real hair, pearly teeth, and sleeping eyes. Phoebe had seen such a doll in radiant dreams; she never expected to have one of her own. Phoebe kept the doll always, with its cherished jointed kid body, exquisitely made German head, even long after its bright 1890s clothes had become quaint. For a long time after the visitor was gone, Phoebe sat in her little rocking chair and held the big doll.

She felt as if any more happiness would destroy her. She smoothed the brown silk dress with rapturous fingers and touched the black slippers tenderly. Her family must have understood her mood, for she was neither disturbed nor teased. After a while, she looked across at the doll buggy with her five other, more humble children. Phoebe felt herself a traitor. Silently she set the new doll in the corner of the old sofa and began her nightly self-imposed task of undressing and putting to bed the five.

It must have been about this time that the headaches began. Nobody ever knew what caused them, but at increasingly frequent intervals, they descended upon Phoebe, shutting her down with throbbing pain until, worn out with tears and suffering, she slept in exhaustion. The old doctor made a great many trips to the farmhouse. He looked pityingly into Phoebe's face, so white around the mouth, such flaming cheeks. When simpler remedies failed, he resorted to more desperate measures. Phoebe would lift her arm pleadingly for the needle she soon learned would bring relief. Perhaps, by the next morning, she would be herself again, the pain forgotten and busy with her small affairs, happy until another attack overtook her.

The headaches became a part of her life, impossible to escape; therefore, she had to endure them. Phoebe became philosophical about them. It was a matter of arranging her life a little differently so that she could accomplish all the necessary tasks despite headaches. Phoebe merely learned to perform more on her good days so that she need not fall behind because of her handicap. In a sense, they did Phoebe a great service: she learned to endure. The strength to endure was a staff upon which she needed to lean.

Phoebe was a friendly soul and did not always play alone. Beyond the dark path through the oaks lived an English family on an adjoining farm. Three girls approximated Phoebe's age and frequently came to play with her.

Hazel and Florence she liked well enough, but Ruby she adored. She and Ruby saw eye to eye and paired off naturally. They were partners in games, in tests of skill; they imposed their wills on the others. Often these good times were interrupted by the demon headache. Then Phoebe would hurry into the house, climb up on the old sofa and strive with all her might to head off the terror. Sadly she would watch while Hazel, Florence, and Ruby gathered their belongings and took the woodland trail home.

In the opposite direction lived two families, each with a boy near Phoebe's age. Rocky was a husky, overgrown boy from well-to-do parents who adored and spoiled him. Phoebe always came to grief in her encounters with Rocky. He was too much for her, too bursting with energy and life. She rarely escaped the headache on days she played with Rocky. One day the wildness of their play resulted in a broken mirror treasured by Aunt Ettie. Another time Rocky stepped on one of mama's baby chicks. Phoebe never forgot the horror she felt of the crushed chick, still pulsing with life. She ran screaming to the old sofa to bury her head in its comforting cushion; she didn't want to play with Rocky again for a long time.

It was different with Henry. He belonged to a very narrow-minded family; a gentle, ineffectual mother and a braggart father. But Phoebe adored Henry: he was her first love, and she didn't care who knew it. When Henry came to play, she kissed him unashamedly and decided to marry him as soon as she could manage. Henry fell in with all her plans, brought her gifts of wild pinks and purloined cinnamon bark, and returned her childhood kisses. Phoebe was at least ten years old with five years of no notice from Henry before she finally gave him up.

Mama was about to be married again: Phoebe had thought nothing of the kind person who had been calling around somewhat frequently. Even when Mama took drives in his shiny buggy and left her with Aunt Ettie, Phoebe didn't mind. She was a big girl and could be left behind without storms and tears. Besides, this man had a fascinating way of taking striped bags of peanuts and chocolates for Phoebe from various pockets. Phoebe approved of him for other reasons: she had embarrassed Mama by standing, hands behind her, and staring at him steadily for long periods when he first began coming to see Mama. Phoebe couldn't see why Mama minded; she was only finding out things, essential things, about him. By listening and watching, Phoebe determined that Silas Fletcher was a man she could depend on, a man with large charity for human weaknesses, a man of warm and tender affections. How could she tell? Phoebe couldn't have explained, but she knew. And all her further acquaintance with this man bore out her conclusions.

Phoebe didn't mind that Mama was to be married. But she was mightily upset over having to move away. Of course, she had to be with Mama. But she belonged here, too, on this beautiful old farm where all her roots had struck down. She didn't see why Mama shouldn't bring her new husband here and said so. And she thought it was very stupid of the family to be amused at her suggestion. Grandpa once more took his pipe from his mouth and spoke his mind to Mama.

"Why shouldn't you be married; he's a good man, and you'll have a good home." But, here, he turned back to his newspaper, rattled it fiercely, "why should you take the baby? She belongs here."

He retreated from sight and refused to listen to any argument. Uncle Will unexpectedly sided with Grandpa, "You'll probably have another family. How do you know Silas will be good to Phoebe? Leave her here, and you'll take no chances."

Aunt Ettie said nothing. She went limping into the kitchen, and Phoebe found her sitting on the wood box and crying hard. Mama was shocked, "If you think I'd leave my child behind!" No one answered, and Mama said flatly, "Well, I don't have to be married." That brought the family round, as Mama thought it would. After all, he was a good man, and Phoebe did belong to Mama.

"Of course, you'll take her with you," declared Aunt Ettie, limping in hurriedly from the kitchen, "The idea!"

Uncle Will got his hat and started for the barn. "Oh, take her, take her," he fumed, "maybe we'll have some peace and quiet around here," and shot out the door, banging it hard. Pure humbug, as Phoebe very well knew.

Only Grandpa refused to budge. He was deaf and made the most of it, rattling his paper aggressively all the rest of the evening. Phoebe was mightily pleased to be the center of this commotion. It made her feel important and influential, and she smiled in the dark as she lay beside Mama that night, cuddled into the feather mattress atop the big straw tick.

"They all want me," she hummed softly to herself, like a little refrain, "They all want me."

Someone else wanted Phoebe too. Rocky's mother, amply able, offered to adopt Phoebe and bring her up with Rocky as her own child. If Rocky's mother hadn't been such a good friend of the family, Phoebe didn't know what Mama might have said to her. Mama's eyes snapped as she set the table for supper after she had come walking home so fast across the field from Rocky's mother's farm.

"The ideas people get in their heads!" Mama said to Aunt Ettie.

"Oh, she meant well," soothed Aunt Ettie, "She's always wanted a little girl." Phoebe began to see through Mama's anger. She was sitting in her little chair undressing the last of the dolls, and she stopped long enough to remark, "I wouldn't live with that Rocky, anyhow. I'd rather live in a tree." Mama stopped short in the middle of the kitchen, a big milk pitcher in her hand. She made big eyes at Aunt Ettie, who made big eyes back.

"What a child," sighed Mama.

Chapter 8 – New Home

The transition from Grandpa's home to her new home was so smoothly made for Phoebe that she hardly realized the dividing line. One day she played happily under the giant oaks. Very soon afterward, she played happily under a big grape arbor fitted with two lovely benches perfect for her housekeeping. She continued to approve of her new papa. He was much older than Mama, but that didn't seem to matter. Mama was very efficient and business-like in her new home. There was a great deal of work for her, even with the help of the hired girl; there were always hired men to feed and make beds for on this big farm. The household was astir early in the morning, with a big breakfast to cook and serve. Phoebe settled herself and her family of dolls tidily into the busy home.

There was one sharp struggle when she insisted on sleeping in Mama's bed.

"Oh, let her sleep where she wants to. She's so little," pleaded Papa.

But Mama said, "She's too big to want her way about everything." She took Phoebe's hand and led her to the little bed in the same room.

"This is your bed, Phoebe, all to yourself. You are to sleep here, and I don't want to hear any more about it."

Phoebe squared her shoulders around independently and looked at Papa. He was sitting on the edge of the big bed, looking as if Mama had scolded him. His eyes were begging Phoebe not to quarrel with Mama. Phoebe suddenly vaulted into the middle of her little bed, shoes and all, and began bouncing high.

"It's a better bed, anyhow," announced Phoebe emphatically, feeling as if she had almost turned defeat into victory by her rapid about-face.

Dan and August were two of Papa's hired men. They were German-born, spoke a broken English that fascinated Phoebe, and were prodigious workers. Phoebe liked August more than Dan. She found out that Dan was selfish and that he played mean tricks. One day she found a great pile of eggs hidden away in the horse barn, and she carried this interesting news item to Papa. The horse barn was Dan's particular territory since he had the care of all the horses on the farm. Papa and Phoebe secured a large milk pail from the porch, slipped into the barn, and carried away all the eggs. This was fun for Phoebe. They did not say a word at the supper table, but Phoebe couldn't eat for staring at Dan and Papa, and she knew Dan had stolen those eggs. He was so obviously perplexed and restless. Phoebe kept a sharp watch on the hiding place after that, but no more eggs were missing.

Another time Papa sent Dan to hitch the light team to the carriage for a trip to town. Dan used the old tarnished harness and kept the lovely new harness for his work team. For once, Papa spoke his mind; Phoebe watched a frightened and chastened Dan change the harness in quick double time.

Chapter 9 – The Surprise

Phoebe

The specter of school was closing in on Phoebe, and she fought it off with all her strength. She didn't want to hear a word about school; she knew she'd hate it, and if she could keep from thinking about it, perhaps it wouldn't overtake her. Because she was tiny and had so many headaches, Mama let her sixth-year slip by with no mention of school. Now she began talking to Phoebe of school.

"All little girls must go to school sometime, Phoebe," she said, "I'm sure you'll like to go once you've started."

Phoebe began crying desperately. How could she make Mama understand this ungovernable dread? She could only mutter, "I won't go to school. I'll never go to school!"

"You are a very naughty girl Phoebe," said Mama. "How would you like to visit Aunt Ettie for a long time this summer?"

"I'd like that," sobbed Phoebe, holding her throbbing head in both hands.

The visit was lovely. Phoebe fell in with all the old ways. Everything was the same; Phoebe galloped joyfully from one dear familiar spot to another and made a brand new playhouse under the cherry tree. She and Grandpa found enough wild strawberries for two pies and a shortcake; Uncle Will let her go barefoot, and Aunt Ettie pieced her a beautiful new quilt for the doll buggy. Two glorious summer months flew by before Mama sent for her. She had forgotten about the school, and she was herself again.

Uncle Will drove old Fanny to take Phoebe back to Mama, and on the way, he said a strange thing, "There's a surprise waiting for you, Phoebe. If you don't like it, come back and live with us."

Phoebe laughed, "I always like surprises."

The surprise was a baby sister, ten days old. Phoebe climbed out of Uncle Will's buggy, flew into the house, and stopped short. Mama was sitting in the big rocking chair, and in her arms, she held this new baby. The baby had black hair and was squalling tempestuously.

Mama said, "Look, Phoebe, a little sister."

Phoebe strolled across the room and stood beside Mama's chair. She looked at Mama, at the new baby, and back at Uncle Will standing in the doorway. The room was very still. Even the baby hushed her cries and seemed to wait for Phoebe to speak.

Then Phoebe said in a low voice, "I think I'll go back with Uncle Will."

But she didn't go back. That night when Mama undressed the baby, she put her in Phoebe's arms, and Phoebe felt her heart melting down to nothing within her. Her thin little arms strained the baby to her.

"You'll have to help me take care of her, Phoebe," declared Mama. "I think she likes you as well as me already."

"It'll be quite a responsibility," sighed Phoebe condescendingly, "but I suppose I'll manage."

Chapter 10 – School

Phoebe went to school, after all. Almost before adjusting to her new niche, she had become a schoolgirl. It was a piece of fortune for her that the new teacher lived with them that year. She was a distant cousin of Papa's; everyone concerned expected her to make her home at the Fletcher farm. Meda Helm was a grave, silent girl. She was recovering from a disastrous love affair, kept her own counsel, and confided in no one. On the first day of school, she and Phoebe walked early to the small white schoolhouse, built a fire, and met the straggling pupils. Phoebe sat, big-eyed and silent, feet dangling, in one of the big double seats. She knew exactly what the situation was: this stern-faced teacher, meeting the curious gaze of the smaller children and the bold stares of the big boys, was a terrified girl. Phoebe was suddenly on her side, both heart and soul. Meda rang the bell from the front door, walked to her desk at the back of the room, and stood stiff and straight until the buzz of voices died. Then she turned, wrote "Meda Helm" on the blackboard, and faced the silent room again.

"I have heard some disturbance and whispering this morning after I rang the bell," she said severely. "There will be no more of that."

Phoebe was smiling secretly, despite her pounding heart. It was a majestic bluff, and it was working, even with the terrible big boys. She would remember the teacher's bluffing, she decided, someday, when she needed to use it.

When the primer class was called to the recitation bench, Phoebe was astounded. These babies couldn't read! She felt some of her timidity oozing away as she listened to the monotonous drill.

"The cat can see the rat. Can the cat get the rat?"

Phoebe had learned to read three years before, as naturally as a flower puts forth its leaves and petals. Uncle Will had given her a Mother Goose for Christmas. She had all the family reading the delightful nonsense to her day after day until she knew every word by heart. The picture on each page was the key. Soon she was sitting in her little rocking chair or on the old sofa, saying the rhymes to herself.

One day she discovered: "Tom, Tom, the Piper's Son," her little finger slipped along the lines. Her heart began beating very rapidly. These strange groups of symbols came out exactly even! She started all over: "Tom, Tom"—why, of course! That was T-O-M, it meant Tom, and there were two of them, therefore, "Tom, Tom!" She went on slowly "the Piper's Son" and on and on to the tune of her beating heart. "Tom went roaring down the street."

She sat very quietly for a long minute. She could read. She could read! Nothing could stop her now. She felt again as she had felt about the birthday doll. It was almost too much happiness; she could scarcely bear so much all at once. Then she was bounding into the old kitchen to throw herself at Mama.

"I can read, look, I can read. Tom, Tom the Piper's Son." Her finger went triumphantly along the lines to the very last word. She and Mama looked at each other.

Finally, Mama said, "Yes, Phoebe, I believe you can read every bit of Mother Goose, but how are you going to read books you haven't memorized?"

But it worked out, after all. Mother Goose, bless her heart, has quite a vocabulary of her own, and soon Phoebe had made that vocabulary hers. Therefore she could read Mother Goose words anyplace. And she wasn't above asking questions, no, indeed! She was soon sitting on Grandpa's lap behind the newspaper, pointing out the Mother Goose words. It was a good game: a word was almost any number of curlicues set apart by spaces. Grandpa got behind on the news while he helped Phoebe play the game. She had a tenacious memory. In a few months, she was reading quite well.

Phoebe

So Phoebe was allowed to pass up the primer and first reader and sit with the second reader class. She thought the second reader very dull, indeed. Her seatmate, jolly Lizzie Smith, had a fourth reader. Phoebe soon had read it through, cover to cover, in her spare moments. Reading was such fun! But arithmetic! Phoebe got her comeuppance in arithmetic, and it was a good thing for Phoebe. It kept her in a healthily chastened mood; maybe she was a prodigy as far as reading went, but her arithmetic was nothing to brag about, and these schoolmates kept her aware of her shortcomings. Nevertheless, she was reasonably happy, made friends, and played hard.

Occasionally and inevitably, she had to go home slowly to live through a bad headache. Only Phoebe knew how long the road home seemed to her at such times. At last, she would arrive, strained white mouth, flaming cheeks, maddening pain. Mama was always her haven; she knew things to do; hot foot baths, cool compresses, sedatives. Sometimes Mama won out, unaided. On a good many other days, as the doctor's horse and buggy stood outside, the whole busy household fretted silently until Phoebe was herself again.

The Oregon country school of the late 1890s was an institution of both good and evil. Good, because at all events, it was a thoroughly democratic concern. Evil in its woeful lack of equipment, it's constantly shifting procession of ill-prepared instructors. But most of all, evil in that it was the perfect spawning ground for mushroom-like growths. And these growths attached themselves to the innocent minds of boys and girls and produced in them strange and unhealthful changes. Most children learned, along with their spelling and first readers, dreadful half-truths about life, particularly about sex. Parents were nicely Victorian, shushing all natural childish inquiries with prudish severity. At school, parental restrictions were removed, and

51

whisperings began seeping downward through the ranks, from the larger and wiser to the smaller and less aware.

One day Lizzie whispered, behind her geography, "Do you know where babies come from?"

"Doctors bring 'em."

"No, they're born; their mothers have 'em."

Phoebe frowned as she washed her slate; this would bear looking into more.

That night Phoebe followed Mama into the bedroom. "What does born mean? Where do babies come from?"

Mama's face turned red. She sang happily to Phoebe;

"Oh, Topsy, she never was bor-r-n,
She never had any mother;
She grew on a pumpkin vine
Just like any other."

Then she began talking very fast about something else. Ah, thought Phoebe, then there was something mysterious about babies. Very well, if Mama wouldn't tell her, she'd find out. Poor Phoebe! She opened her ears to the undercover whispering; she became, in successive stages, horrified, avid, and satiated.

For a while, she avoided Papa and Mama. She looked with dark suspicion upon the genesis of her baby sister; she hated all the boys in school, then grew enormously curious about them. Finally, she knew shame for her thoughts and suffered acutely in her own estimation. The last stage of her disease was a gradual return to a healthier attitude. There were still books to be read, games to play, and folks to love.

Phoebe was out of the shadows, into the sunshine once more, except, ah yes, there were traces left of the poisonous growth; she didn't ask Mama specific questions; she decided never to be married!

Tell me, where does imagination come from? The roots of Phoebe's imaginings must have embedded themselves in strange crannies. Perhaps every child leads a double life; Phoebe certainly did. She went about her small affairs with a serious straightforwardness that disarmed the casual observer. A good share of her life floated like the surface water of a smooth river. She played with her dolls, and she tended conscientiously to her baby sister. She went to school, played, and longed mightily for a bicycle. But she also struggled, daily and nightly, with the problem of salvation, or was it damnation?

She was going to Sunday School now, and Sunday School, with crisp, clean dresses, beflowered hats, a semi-circle of small girls like herself, picnics, and shared secrets, had its certain advantages. Occasionally she stayed for the church service and went home for Sunday dinner with a companion. The sermons were evangelistic and soul-searching.

Phoebe began worrying about her soul. She repeatedly dreamed of a horrific scene in which a very red and personal devil came out of the ground behind the woodshed in the schoolyard and made straight for her despairing self. Satan never quite captured her, for Phoebe always awoke, shrieking wildly, to find Mama or Papa, or sometimes both, pulling her awake to a safe world. She finally solved that particular problem herself. If God was the kind of a God who would let Satan get her when she was so desirous of heaven, then she didn't want anything to do with Him.

"Papa wouldn't let me go to hell, no matter how naughty I was," she reflected. "If God isn't as forgiving as Papa, He doesn't amount to much. If He is, then I don't have to worry." (And she later discovered that He's ever so much more if one chooses that path!) She quit dreaming about the devil. There were other fears not so readily exorcised. Phoebe was terribly afraid of sharp things. Points of needles, pitchforks, rakes, pins, edges of knives, scythes, and broken glass. Just thinking of sharp points of edges gave her a dreadful feeling in the soles of her feet. She tried not to think of knives cutting her feet and succeeded in thinking of them almost constantly.

If she touched her feet to the floor as she sat busy with her lessons at school, she felt the knives slicing through her soles and drew her feet up in a panic. Then she hit upon the expedient of a book under her feet that helped so long as the teacher didn't notice. She began tucking her feet under her whenever she sat down, a foolish and awkward habit that followed her for years and caused her spine to grow just a bit one-sided.

The worst fear of all was suffocation. While she still lived in Grandpa's house, Phoebe got a prune pit lodged in her throat and felt the breath of life denied her for a fearful minute. Mama had grasped the situation and shook Phoebe upside down until the seed flew out of her mouth. Much as she longed to learn to swim, Phoebe was too afraid of the water to venture far. She decided one day, incredibly daring, to cure herself of this fear of water. She filled a basin with water, stood before it drawing long precious breaths, then plunged her face to the bottom of the pan. The cure wasn't successful. She had forgotten to hold her breath.

Chapter 11 - Helen

The little half-sister had been named Helen. Phoebe liked the name; Phoebe was reading voraciously now, anything she could lay her hands on, and somewhere she had learned about that other Helen, Helen of Troy, a mythical beauty whose face was said to have "launched a thousand ships" in the Trojan War thousands of years ago. Phoebe's sister, little Helen, had a face to be reckoned with, too. She had darker brown eyes than Phoebe's, and her dark hair curled in soft tendrils. These desirable attributes were Phoebe's envy and still her true delight. She mourned again before the mirror over her deficiencies while busily training Helen's ringlets into real curls.

Papa was enormously proud of this new daughter born in his fiftieth year. But he was proud of Phoebe, too. He gloried in her reading precocity and helped her with the worrisome arithmetic. Together he and Phoebe had Helen walking when she was eleven months. As for talking, Helen needed no help with that! She had burst into speech at an incredibly early age. Her personality was an aggressive one: she took her place very soon in the exact center of the household, the members of which revolved willingly around her.

Papa had bought Helen the tiniest pair of rubber boots in town. Helen and her fairy boots were a precious combination; they were apt to turn up together in any corner of the farm at the most unexpected moments. Because she was afraid of nothing, everyone constantly had to rescue her from dangerous pursuits. She walked unconcernedly beneath the bellies of the horses; she entered the stall of the Jersey bull, a fearful creature, and was hauled to safety by a disgusted farmhand.

In a single day during which she had been left in Phoebe's care, she besmeared herself successively with ink, blackberries, and kerosene. She was never still; her tiny feet were constantly running, and her active voice kept up with her running feet. When she had completely exhausted herself, she fell asleep in whatever spot she happened to be, whence Phoebe would carry her back to the house and her waiting bed.

One of the hired men was a Spanish war veteran. Will Durant, probably 24 years old, had a gift for narrative, and his stories of adventures in the Philippines held the family spellbound on many a winter evening. He had a large box filled with trophies which he displayed. Phoebe would handle them breathlessly: strings of heavy beads; unusual knives and wicked-looking swords; strange coins; a braid of coarse black hair, and the odor that arose from these unfamiliar objects was the weirdest thing. It belonged to another world than Phoebe's. It spelled fear and danger and sent shivers over her body.

Phoebe often climbed into the lap of whichever man was handiest—Papa, preferably, except that now she must share that lap with Helen. Dan and August often held her, and sometimes she scrambled onto Will's lap when a good story was in progress. Mama's current hired girl, Phoebe discovered, was blushing and casting her eyes down before the dashing Will. Phoebe understood that Emma was falling in love with Will and the thought made Phoebe furious. She decided to put her finger in this pie and waylaid Will on his way to the barn.

"Do you like Emma?" she demanded without preamble and was gratified to observe that her onset was causing Will some confusion. But he was a straightforward creature and answered Phoebe honestly enough.

"Emma is a nice girl; yes, I like her..." Then he bent his dark brows upon Phoebe, "You're a funny little girl; why do you ask?"

Phoebe was furious. "I'm not funny! I'm nine years old. Are you going to marry her?"

Will laughed, a great shout, "Marry Emma? Of course not, honey! I'm not going to marry anybody. Then I couldn't spend as much time with you and the family."

Phoebe was delighted. She felt very compassionate toward Emma, and she smiled about it for at least a week when she forgot all about Will and took up some new enthusiasm.

In the little Baptist Sunday School Phoebe attended stood a high bookcase filled with rows of drab-colored books. When Phoebe discovered these books could be had for the asking, she launched herself into a veritable orgy of reading.

Every Sunday, she carried home two books, lost herself entirely for hours at a time in their pages, invariably read them through, and brought home two more on the following Sunday. The books were the usual Sunday School variety, highly moral in tone and horrific in plot. They dealt with themes of inheritance, temperance, and temptation. Phoebe believed everything she read and remembered every character. Reading drove her into herself; the actual world around her withdrew to a great distance when Phoebe read: sometimes, it disappeared entirely. At such times, if Mama called her to run an errand, she was roused with difficulty and went unwillingly.

"Phoebe-with-her-nose-in-a-book" came to be accepted in the family and left, for the most part, to her resources. When Helen had her fourth birthday, Phoebe realized that Mama was to have another baby. Something of the old horror returned to her. She felt hot and ashamed when she saw the hired men glance at Mama. Once, she overheard a sly remark that sent her boiling with anger to Mama. But she couldn't tell; after all, she could only sob and beg that Dan be sent away "for keeps."

"I hate him!"

Papa was very concerned and tried his best to get to the real reason for Phoebe's concern, but Phoebe only shook her head and said again, "He talks horrid. I hate him!"

Chapter 12 - Baby William

One morning when Phoebe came to breakfast, she stopped short in the middle of the big dining room. In the old rocking chair outside of Mama's door lay a soft bundle, and it was moving a bit. Phoebe crept closer and peered into a very red and wrinkled little face. Yes, sure enough, the doctor's voice in the bedroom, his horse and buggy tied outside, a strange woman being bossy about the house.

When Helen discovered the baby, she created a considerable commotion. Under cover of Helen's noisy questions and comments, Phoebe learned that the new arrival was a boy who weighed ten pounds. A little later, she stood by Mama's bed, asking to be allowed to stay home from school.

"Do you have a headache?"

Phoebe wished her head did ache. Why didn't it hurt when it would do her some good? She could only shake the offending head in denial.

"Then go along to school, Phoebe. You can see the new baby when you get home."

Phoebe was thinking of the boys and girls at school: their sly eyes, their whispers. "But I don't have to tell them," she thought, suddenly, and went off docilely. All day her secret lay heavy on her mind. What would they say when they did find out, as they surely would by tomorrow? In desperation, she whispered her secret to Lizzie, the constant seat-mate, as they put their books away for dismissal.

"I don't want the kids to know I have a baby."

"We'll tell 'em tomorrow, and I'll shush anyone who dares laugh," hissed Lizzie.

But it wasn't so bad after all. Outside in the cold November rain, Will Durant waited on Papa's most handsome pony, sent by Papa and Mama to bring Phoebe home. He smiled condescendingly at the ring of Phoebe's schoolmates gathered about as he settled Phoebe before him.

"Not every girl can have a bouncing ten-pound brother," he declared, "Best looking baby I've seen in a long spell." Realizing from the blank faces that he had told a secret Phoebe had chosen to keep, he came nobly to her defense.

"'Course Phoebe wouldn't be bragging, even when she had a right to tell. Get up, Bess!" Down the road, they went at a smart clip, Phoebe's rubber boots kicking up and down. She felt warm and comforted inside. That was the way to get hard things done! Make believe you liked 'em. She hummed all the way home and decided to bring up the baby brother so as to avoid all the blunders she had committed with Helen.

But bringing up the baby brother devolved upon Mama and Mama alone. For all his ten-pound start in life, little William barely held his own the first few months. There was constant difficulty with his feedings. His head grew, but his starved body became a pitiful sight. Mama and Papa agonized over him. The household feared to hope since hope seemed so vain. At last, the baby got a toehold on life, a slender one but tenacious. He grew, but so very slowly. When he finally walked by himself, one fearful hand reaching backward to Papa while the other strained toward Mama's outstretched arms, Phoebe, for the first time, believed that William would grow up. He was so different from the aggressive Helen: his world was so full of fears, the shadows so black that his eyes always seemed strained wide in alarm.

Phoebe loved William from the beginning; she learned to be very patient with his fretfulness, carrying him from room to room, wherever Mama went.

William was frantic when Mama was out of his sight for a moment. Mama grew heavy-eyed from worry and sleeplessness, but she never grew discouraged. Mama brought William through, but she always said that Phoebe was her right-hand girl.

Chapter 13 - Town

Phoebe

When Papa decided to sell the big farm and move into town, Phoebe and Helen were wildly excited. It had become impossible for Mama to carry the heavy load of farmhouse work and give proper care to the delicate William. It was a good farm, and prospective buyers were not hard to find. It was Phoebe's first actual move that she was involved in, and the preparations were fascinating. Papa had bought a feed mill and store on the edge of town and secured a comfortable house for the family. Phoebe confided in Lizzie that she didn't think much of the idea of a town school. The arithmetic in town school was likely too daunting, and the kids were standoffish.

"And what will I wear?" she moaned.

"Aprons," said Lizzie.

"Oh, mercy, not aprons! In town, you have to dress up every day."

The move was finally accomplished, and the family settled in the new home. It seemed strange not to have Dan, August, Will, and a hired girl around the table. Just Papa, Mama, Phoebe, Helen, and little William in his baby carriage, watching Mama's every move, tracking her with wide-open eyes.

But Phoebe didn't go to school until the following fall. It was a bad smallpox year in town, and Mama feared Phoebe would be exposed. It was a welcome reprieve to Phoebe, to whom town school had been a cause of bad dreams.

The bad dreams almost came true when Phoebe started to attend school the following fall. Because she hailed from an ungraded country school, she had to be put through her paces before they would assign her to the proper room. The reading went splendidly. Barnes' Fourth Reader she knew thoroughly, and she read well, even when fear held her hands as they rigidly grasped her book. The principal ushered her into the third-grade room. He was a fearsome man with staring brown eyes. The teacher was Miss Starr, a severe-looking woman with neat

64

blond hair and bitter lines around her firm mouth. First, Phoebe read from the Third reader, then from the Fourth. This wasn't hard; she took courage, a new breath, and launched into "When Freedom from her mountain height" to the end. She put her book down and looked fearfully into the two silent faces above her. The principal cleared his throat noisily. "Very good, very good indeed, Miss Starr. Test her on arithmetic and use your judgment," and moved on to weightier matters than Phoebe.

Miss Starr began with the multiplication tables. Phoebe knew them; she knew them all. She knew the combinations almost as well because she had a good memory. Then Miss Starr put mental arithmetic into her hand and set her a problem. Phoebe went promptly to pieces, couldn't think, and dissolved into shamed tears. Miss Starr looked at the door through which Mr. Graham had gone, looked down on the despairing Phoebe, and smiled gravely.

"All right, Phoebe, I think you belong in the fourth grade," she said briskly, "Try hard with your arithmetic, and don't be afraid of anyone."

She took Phoebe's cold hand in hers and led her across the hall into the fourth-grade room.

"Miss Bellinger, this Phoebe Miller; she is going to be one of your girls."

The bell downstairs rang, and Phoebe knew that the room would soon be full of strange boys and girls. She looked desperately into Miss Bellinger's face and took heart, for it was the kindest face in the world, young and beautiful, with soft brown eyes, wavy auburn hair, and a generous peppering of freckles.

She settled Phoebe into a seat of her own with a few deft motions and stood beside her as the double line of fourth graders marched in and found seats. Then she said casually, a firm hand on Phoebe's shoulder, "This is Phoebe, a new girl; you are all to help make her feel at home in the fourth grade."

So Phoebe crossed another bridge. The dreaded first day of school cost Phoebe a terrific headache and Mama hours of lost sleep that night, but the next morning Phoebe was up promptly, eager to become a part of this new school world. She loved her teacher, and she could read with the best of them. Phoebe had been smiled at by the other little girls and looked over by all the boys, and she'd get that nasty mental arithmetic if she had to stay up nights. She felt she had met the challenge so far and belonged.

Chapter 14 – The Bargain

One night when Phoebe came home from school, she missed Helen's eager face peering for her over the gate top. Helen's impatience barely survived the long school day until Phoebe was back home, and she would climb the gate and peer up the road until Phoebe's red jacket came into view.

Tonight Phoebe found Mama very concerned over Helen, who lay on the sofa, shaking with a chill and demanding more and more covers, then petulantly throwing them off, declaring she was burning up. Before midnight the doctor had paid a visit and uttered a dreadful word "pneumonia."

Helen grew steadily worse, Phoebe was kept home from school, and one night the doctor stayed all through the night, fighting to keep Helen alive. Phoebe joined the battle once more against death. She carried little William from room to room, tended him, and cared for him faithfully since Mama could not. But with all her strength, she was pushing once more to keep out a dark enemy.

She turned to God, not humbly a supplicant, but demandingly. She reminded God that Papa was a good man, that Mama had had trouble enough, and that this threatened blow would be unfair, and shameful. She saw the fear and anguish in these beloved faces, and she fell to bargaining with God.

"If you let Helen get well, I'll get the highest grades in school this year, despite mental arithmetic," she promised, and added for good measure, "and won't whisper once in school hours, all year. Amen."

It was Phoebe's covenant and the best she could do. She tried to have faith that God would hear and answer, and she finally slept. Sometime before morning, she stole downstairs and crept into Mama's room.

The doctor still sat by Helen's bed; Mama and Papa sat on the other side, watching the doctor as Phoebe cuddled between them. The lamp was turned down and gave only a feeble light, but the little fireplace had a bed of coals that gleamed redly.

Poor Helen lay gasping and spent, and the doctor was doing swiftly what he could do. Phoebe could almost hear the beating of dark wings, but she strove against them. She demanded a miracle of God.

And God heard, for the doctor was bending closely over Helen now, and he reached and turned the lamp higher. He drew his fingers over Helen's forehead, sighed deeply, and let his big shoulders sag. He turned to smile at Mama and Papa.

"I think she's going to make it," he whispered, "she's better."

Phoebe never remembered any more of that night. Papa and Mama told her they had found her later asleep in the very middle of the bed and that when Papa had carried her upstairs and tucked her in, she hadn't awakened, but she had muttered in her sleep, "I will get that mental arithmetic, God."

Papa thought it was a good joke on Phoebe, and Phoebe let it go at that. School claimed Phoebe again, school and home, play, and mental arithmetic! She struggled with it daily, she dreamed dreadfully of it by night, and the textbook traveled to and from school until its covers loosened and all but fell away. It was hard and discouraging. She would tackle the problems at night, marshaling the figures in her mind until she could put her book behind her and talk her way triumphantly to the correct conclusion.

But it was much harder at school with everyone listening and her heart beating so madly with fright. Suddenly she began to make a go of it. Soon she was a match for any girl in the fourth grade in mental arithmetic, and then she deliberately invaded the boys' territory, determined to be victorious there as well. Because she read well and remembered readily, her other classes gave her no trouble.

She concentrated on mental arithmetic and James. For James McAlpin was the acknowledged champion.

Report cards came out, and Phoebe's grades were good. She wished that she could see James McAlpin's mental arithmetic grade, but she wouldn't ask, for James had little use for girls in general.

For Phoebe, in particular, who was crowding him from his pedestal, he had only a considerable contempt. Phoebe and James went at it again, each with equal and enthusiastic backing. Miss Ballinger took advantage of the situation to arrange a contest extending through the last weeks of school.

James and Phoebe selected their teammates, and the teacher kept the score. Phoebe remembered her promise to God and worked as she never had before. She memorized pages of review problems; she practiced them over at home as she carried William about. Phoebe continued with them after she was in bed.

The promise not to whisper was easy. Phoebe wouldn't do that under any circumstances, and soon her peculiarity came to be taken for granted. The conflict of mental arithmetic forces grew hotter; the lines wavered, advanced, and retreated, with the honors first with Phoebe, then with James. Phoebe grew desperate: she began coaching her weaker adherents, came early, stayed late, and used up her noon hour.

On the last day of the contest, Phoebe was so tired she lost all count of points. She only knew she had to win because of her earlier "bargain" with God.

The problems went up and down the contesting lines, thinning the ranks until only Phoebe and James were left, as usual. The room was hushed as the teacher added up the final points.

"I am thrilled over the results of this contest," said Miss Ballinger, "because neither side won, and both sides won. The contest is a tie."

Phoebe felt very bewildered. Under cover of the shout that went up, she stole a look at James. He was looking at her and smiling broadly, Phoebe smiled back, but her thoughts were whirling. This was terrible! She felt on probation with God,

While she piled her books to take home, the teacher passed the report cards. Phoebe picked hers up abstractedly, saw it was good, and with one corner of her mind, heard the teacher saying, "I wish everyone a happy vacation. You will be interested to know that Phoebe, by a narrow margin, made the highest grades for the year. She and James are the champions again."

Something burst like a skyrocket in Phoebe's mind. Grades, of course! This thing hadn't depended on mental arithmetic alone. She'd promised God to get the highest grades. She slid off probation and went whooping joyfully after the rest of the fourth graders toward home and vacation.

From the vantage point of her maturer years, Phoebe could look back over the vista of her life. Her tree of life seemed to have its deepest roots in Dr. Moors Farwell. Perhaps that was wishful thinking, the beginning she would have chosen; still, she knew that in her veins ran the bloodstreams of many other, and probably less desirable, donors. Someone indeed was responsible for her nameless childish fears, dark days and her bright ones, her unreasonable capacity for being wounded by small causes. These unlovely traits she recognized early and strove furiously against their influence. But her efforts to uproot and cast out these unattractive aspects of herself were, for the most part, impotent.

Since Dr. Moors was only one root from which to draw strength for her battle toward a better-balanced personality, she must necessarily do what she could with the material at hand, for Phoebe strove toward a shining and impossible goal of perfection. Even as a child, she loved the beauty of line and proportion. At five years, she had watched with ecstasy the filmy edges of clouds slip across a blue June sky. She knew the pattern that bursting oak leaves make in spring. She loved and handled the small perfections of wild strawberry blossoms and the pattern on the June bug's back delicately. And the feelings! And sensations! The feel against her fingers of the velvet on her red dress and the lovely plush on Mama's album she never forgot. Words and phrases called up images of sheer beauty.

An old hymn beginning:
I will sing you a song of that beautiful land
The faraway home of the soul;
Where storms never beat on the glittering sand,
And the years of eternity roll.
(Ecclesiastics, "Ere Ever Yet the Silver Cord")

This hymn fascinated Phoebe. She sang it over and over to herself, feeling those endless years of eternity rolling over her until the pleasure seemed overwhelming. She ran to Mama to stop the dreadful inevitability of the force she had set in motion.

During adolescence, Phoebe put away some things, never to haunt her again. She was done with thoughts of eternal punishment, terrors, and fears of sharp points and cutting edges. These bogies she had battled and put to rout. Some others she kept and, as might be expected, still others she acquired. Her roots seemed to extend into a trunk which became a more unified personality expressed as the consistent persona that she presented to her friends and, later on, her family.

Chapter 15 - Bill

At thirteen years, Phoebe became aware of boys in a somewhat different sense than she had considered them earlier. In the country, schoolboys had pulled her braids and stolen her rubber boots. In town, James McAlpin had openly scorned her, along with all the other little girls, to be sure, and they had cordially detested him in return.

Now Phoebe, to her amazement and self-distrust, suddenly found herself thinking a great deal indeed about a certain boy. Not James McAlpin, but another boy in her seventh grade, Bill Davis, a great hulk of a boy with a slow good-natured grin and a decidedly inferior report card rating. Phoebe took to analyzing, parsing, and diagramming in her English class with half a mind, so to speak, while the remaining lobe concentrated on Bill. He sat two seats in front of her, one row over. She knew exactly how the part in his black wavy hair detoured around a cowlick in the front and ended in a double crown in the back. She knew the thumbnail of his left hand was turning black, and a new one was replacing it, and she had discovered with secret amusement that one ear was set a bit higher than the other. Bill had blue eyes and a drawling voice, enormous feet, and beautiful freckles. In fact, he was altogether adorable, and Phoebe hated herself for liking him.

She wanted dreadfully to talk to Mary about Bill. Mary was Phoebe's chum, a year younger, in the same grade. She lived in the same block and was a most satisfactory confidante. Mary was blond, as were her German parents; she was calm, judicial, and friendly. Mary planted her feet on firm earth, and she kept them there. She regarded Phoebe's wild flights of imagination with wonder and patience in her blue eyes.

All day long at school, Mary plodded at her lesson, twisting and untwisting a lock of fair curly hair over one ear. She sat opposite Phoebe, and each girl knew unerringly what the other was doing, almost what she was thinking. Phoebe knew that Mary would soon be aware of Phoebe's interest in Bill, and she dreaded that time to come, for Mary was still serenely unaware of boys. True, she played with them, quarreled with them, and dealt with boys at every turn, but still, she didn't think about them. Phoebe wished she didn't.

Some of the older girls were frankly boy-struck. They came to school smelling sweet of their mother's forbidden perfume and bedaubed with talcum powder. Talcum powder was the very most a little girl might do in the way of elegant makeup. Fine rice face powder was not considered appropriate, and rouge was acknowledged only in awed whispers. Phoebe sometimes begged for a bit of Mama's violet talcum powder but was admonished to wait awhile longer. As a special favor, Mama allowed her a drop of lily of the valley perfume on her handkerchief occasionally. She had been using quite a lot lately, but it hadn't seemed to make the slightest impression on Bill. Phoebe wasn't sure she wanted that to happen, anyway.

Sometimes Phoebe stopped on the fringes of the bigger girl groups to listen to the conversation. She knew the girls often carried notes from the boys and received gifts of gum and candy from their particular beaux. Phoebe wasn't much impressed by what she heard. She had a feeling that all this was beside the point and that she was searching for something that she would never find in the callow confidence of these girls. She felt restless, disturbed, impatient, and unsettled.

Phoebe hadn't the slightest idea what Bill could possibly have to do with her discomfort. Groping for a solution to this new disturbance, she decided to do a bold thing. Phoebe would send Bill Davis a valentine! On the way home from school, she and Mary stopped at the stationery store and looked over the valentine stock. Phoebe failed to find, in all the conglomerate, anything that, to any degree, carried a message she would care to send to Bill, and she almost chucked the idea altogether. But not entirely.

A few evenings later, she had collected sundry materials together, and one Saturday afternoon, she crept into the loft of Papa's feed store under the gable window. It smelled lovely in here of baled hay and dusty sunshine. Papa would gladly have allowed Phoebe the use of his tiny office downstairs: there was a big sloping desk and high stool and plenty of light, but there wasn't privacy. Helen had the run of the office and a magpie's propensities for discovering Phoebe's whereabouts and undertakings, but she hadn't found the retreat under the gable window. Then, on a prone bale of hay, Phoebe spread out her materials: a bottle of paste, pen, and ink—red ink! Scissors, a double sheet of secretly borrowed paper from Papa's desk, a sheet of long cherished silver foil, and a piece of bright red paper from the art supply at school. But the most beautiful of all was a strip of lace paper taken from the inside of an empty candy box.

Phoebe's conscience smote her a little because of the red paper: it was a piece apportioned to her use last art lesson; still, one wasn't supposed to bring materials home. She hardened her heart, nevertheless. This was an extraordinary occasion, and if God was watching her, He could remember the mental arithmetic three years ago! So Phoebe worked happily, humming a little.

Phoebe forgot everything except the joy of creation; she even forgot Bill. She exerted herself to the utmost to make a beautiful valentine; she put a bit of her being into the making, and the little verse she penned and tucked into the finished product was as pretty, as chaste and cool, as snow. Lastly, she fashioned an envelope to fit the valentine, sealed it, and printed on it, Mr. Bill Davis.

The valentine reposed safely in Bill's geography book. Phoebe had managed well, and she had had luck; after everyone had left for home the day before, Phoebe had slipped upstairs into the empty room, put the white envelope in the geography book at tomorrow's lesson and hurried down again to the waiting Mary. It was a shame not to tell Mary, reflected Phoebe, but somehow she couldn't.

Phoebe made absent-minded replies to Mary's observations, wondering how she'd ever endure seeing Bill find the valentine. She didn't believe she could bear it; maybe she'd better have a headache! But she knew she wouldn't miss being there. Far ahead, she could see Bill, and even a distant view of his dark head made Phoebe anxious. She loitered along, turning her sensations over in her mind, taking them apart and examining them minutely. She didn't enjoy feeling secretive and curious about Bill, but she was intensely interested in her reactions. Here was something to be watched, something that had a moving force that carried her along willy-nilly, made her self-conscious, awkward, and at the same time, immensely aware of herself. And even as she assented to Mary's proposal to a round-about way home to look for spring beauties in the oak grove, she was smiling a little to herself over the futility of the wasted lily of the valley perfume.

All her life and with varying emotions, Phoebe could stand back and watch herself at the crossroads of her journey. She was something of a fatalist because she believed her own decisions were inevitable. Although she owned the unwise ones, she felt that if there could ever be a second chance, her feet would follow the same paths. She could and did look back with laughter, shame, pain, and amusement, but she could not second-guess her past decisions.

Helen was skittering in and out of Phoebe's room, her brown eyes bright as stars, her short skirts flying. As Phoebe struggled with her coiffeur before her beloved bird's eye maple dresser, she kept twisting her neck to observe Helen. Helen was seven now, in the second grade. She took life in large luscious doses and digested it with carefree ease.

She was vivid and assertive; something always happened when Helen was around, and she did get around. In her joyful abandon, Helen reminded Phoebe of a Mother Goose character who rode on a white horse while shaking the "rings on her fingers and bells on her toes." This morning she finally stopped long enough to prop her elbows on the dresser and watch with intense interest as the last hairpins secured the stubborn, fly-away coiffeur.

As Phoebe fluffed out the enormous black taffeta bow tied to the top of her braid, Helen asked, "you like Bill Davis, don't you?"

Two pairs of brown eyes met in the glass, and Phoebe saw her reflected face turning a dreadful red. This wretched Helen! She shan't know, thought Phoebe; it isn't fair for Helen to snoop like this; if I don't settle her now, I'll never have any privacy or peace. She continued gazing sternly at Helen in the glass for a moment, noting with distaste her teasing grin. Then she turned with great dignity and stalked to the head of the stairs.

"Mama!" she shouted, "Listen, Mama! Helen is a horrible nuisance. She won't stay out of my room, Mama!" Her voice sounded choked and strained and overloud.

What in the world! Phoebe heard Mama coming closer to the foot of the stairs.

"Why, Phoebe! Does it matter if Helen comes into your room?" Mama stood now where Phoebe could see her, and she had a look of amazement on her face.

"You'd better hurry; Mary is waiting out front."

Helen had come up behind Phoebe, twitching her braid, and chanted loudly, "She likes Bill Davis, Mama; she loves Bill Davis, Mama!"

A fit of mighty anger raised Phoebe's chest and shot sparks from her eyes. She waited for two breaths for Mama to tend to Helen. Mama was smiling; her eyes were teasing, like Helen's. Phoebe turned on Helen, smacked her hard, first on one red cheek, then on the other, then rushed past Mama in shame and rage to meet Mary at the front gate.

Phoebe continued feeling furious with Helen all day, but she felt almost as angry with herself. She knew her resentment was out of all proportion to the offense, and she couldn't understand why that was so. Helen had often teased her; she had never before felt so devastated with burning anger. She began analyzing again: is it because of Bill? No, not really, because Helen doesn't know how I feel about Bill; I don't know myself. I don't care if Helen comes into my room. What I don't want is for Helen to go into my mind or wherever it is since that is my own and where no one else has a right to be. I belong to myself, raged Phoebe. Neither Helen nor anyone has a right to surprise me in my innermost thoughts. I won't have it! I can't have it because when that happens, it destroys me, too. This inner tumult went forward all day.

Phoebe could struggle with herself while she parsed and diagrammed, recited the machinations of the circulatory system glibly, and intoned "An Incident of the French Camp" in an acceptable sort of detachment.

In a fine sort of aloofness, Phoebe watched Bill find his valentine. There was something more important on her mind. By the time school was dismissed, she felt a measure of peace. She knew there would have to be an accounting with Mama, and she doubted if she could make her understand; therefore, she felt dread of the ordeal. But she would have a try at it, anyway.

She loitered until Bill was some distance ahead before she started home, her arm tight around Mary's loyal waist. Each girl had a bundle of valentines from the box at school. They had examined them critically before leaving the classroom and had discovered the authorship of most unerringly. Phoebe had no valentine from Bill: she felt a strange twisting ache over this fact; probably, she reflected darkly, he would never know that she had labored over the most handsome one in his collection. She watched his tall form disappear around a turn in the road, and she almost decided to give him up forever.

At the front gate, she parted from Mary with unusual affection and plans for after supper. Now, she thought, as she marched up to the door, I'm in for it! Her heart began thumping tremendously. I must make Mama see that Helen must not pry into my business. But of course, I shouldn't have slapped her: I'll tell Mama I know better than to do that and that I'm sorry.

Phoebe stopped short at the top step, for there lay a huge white envelope with "Phoebe" on it, in Bill's handwriting. With cold fingers, she drew out a queenly valentine, a super beautiful valentine. So he had done it, after all! Suddenly she understood: everything was crystal clear. He liked her all along! She had no burden of unrequited love to bear, no hurt pride to hide. She tucked the valentine into its envelope and went humming in search of Mama and whatever punishment was in store for her.

Eighth-grade activities were filling every moment of Mary's and Phoebe's lives. Surprise parties were the great social diversion: Mary and Phoebe had taken their turns at being surprised by some thirty classmates. On such occasions, the kitchen table was piled high with the sandwiches supplied by the boys' mothers and the cakes, rivaling masterpieces of the girls' mothers' culinary abilities.

Chocolate and homemade ice cream usually were the contribution of the hostess, and the more generous souls extended themselves to provide potato salad and pickles. As for paper napkins! In this field, the mothers let themselves go. They did not put paper napkins to practical use. True, they rested for a fleeting moment on crisply starched laps of the girls and serge-clad best-suit knees of the boys. But after supper, each napkin made the rounds of the party and was duly inscribed with the names and often the sentiments of the assembled guests. Phoebe cherished, for many years, a collection of these gala remembrances.

Parties usually began with very innocent diversions. Parlor tricks were popular for a starter, games in which two initiated leaders puzzled the wits of the others. Gradually the ranks of the puzzled thinned as they deciphered the "code." After an hour of such preliminaries, the party found a faster tempo, and the demand for "Wink'em," voiced first by the bolder, soon found agreement with the other adolescents.

Phoebe found herself since Valentine's Day openly accepted in the crowd as Bill's girl. Now he assumed masterful airs as he successfully kept Phoebe in the chair in front of him despite beckoning winks from those who tried to draw her away as was the object of the "Wink'em" game. It was exciting for Phoebe to be the center of attention; it made her feel grown up. Her eyes sparkled as she heard Bill's drawling, "What's all the hurry, Phoebe?" or "Sit down and stay awhile, Phoebe." The Wink'em beckoners didn't stand a chance since Phoebe only had eyes for Bill.

At recess one Wednesday, Bill asked Phoebe if he could take her to Mary's surprise party the following Friday.

"I'll ask Mama," promised Phoebe breathlessly.

This would be fun! She would wear her best new hair ribbon and her pink dress. Phoebe wished she had a new pair of slippers. She'd ask Mama for those, too, or perhaps she had better ask Papa first; that would likely be wiser. Mama might think her old slippers are quite nice enough for neighborhood parties.

But if she were going with Bill—! She hurried Mary home, successfully evaded all her speculation about the next party, and burst in on Mama.

"Mama, Bill asked to take me to Mary's party. May I go with him, Mama? Oh, please, Mama! Really, all the girls go with someone."

Mama looked very doubtful.

"You are only a little girl, Phoebe," she said anxiously. "Papa and I had hoped you wouldn't want to go with the boys just yet—and besides," Mama began laughing a little, "after all, it's only three blocks to Mary's house. Surely you can go that far alone." She looked lovingly, coaxingly, at Phoebe.

Phoebe felt herself giving in to Mama, even while she cherished the picture of herself, splendid in pink dress and new slippers, opening the door to Bill's knock.

"Well," she said slowly, "if you think I oughtn't, Mama," and started for the kitchen with her lunch box. And then Mama did a splendid, a gallant right about face. She stopped Phoebe and, speaking very fast, almost as if afraid of not getting it said in time, gave Phoebe her permission to go with Bill. She did even better; she promised Phoebe a new dress besides the new slippers. Phoebe was in a dither of joy. It was so good of Mama to make everything so beautiful for Phoebe's first date.

Papa was very humorous over Phoebe and Bill, and Helen had the curiosity that nearly killed a cat. Mama had made the new dress, white dotted swiss, with puff sleeves and a full skirt. Mama was very tired, but she was almost as excited as Phoebe, who was allowed, as a crowning concession, a light dusting of Mama's powder. Perfumed and beautiful, she greeted Bill, resplendent in his turn in the best suit and

lovely blue necktie, and unmanageable hair firmly chastened. So
Phoebe, the blessings of her family on her head, walked with Bill the
three blissful blocks to Mary's party.

Parlor tricks and Wink'em followed the small flurry Phoebe and
Bill's coincident arrival caused. The party progressed to Clap-in-and-
Clap-out and arrived inevitably at Post-office. Phoebe had been kissed
before in these experimental adolescent games; the kisses hadn't stirred
her particularly. Some boys disgusted her, rough shoving and
manhandling in a dark hall. A favored few with the girls had a certain
finesse, an immature gallantry that had its appeal to romantic minds.

Bill had never kissed Phoebe. While she waited for her name,
Phoebe had a trembling expectancy of something different, something
that would be a fulfillment of dreams. She slipped from the bright
living room of Mary's house into the dim hall, accompanied by much
immature humor.

"Now," thought Phoebe, "I'll find out: I'll know in a minute whether
Bill is different." The door closed; she couldn't see or hear. Where was
Bill?

"Oh, I don't want to! I'm afraid! Let me out!" cried Phoebe's heart.
She braced herself, shrinking against the wall. Then she felt Bill's big
hand on her shoulder, not rough or shoving, not hot or clutching, but
quiet and almost timid. She stood very still, waiting, her face half-
averted.

She smelled the lovely bay rum on Bill's hair and felt the softest of
kisses on her temple. That was all. She drew a long relieved breath,
heard Bill chuckle, and joined him wholeheartedly as they both
stepped hesitantly back into the light.

It was over, and there hadn't been anything, either good or bad.
Phoebe was happy she decided not to grow up just yet. She wasn't very

wise, but she did realize a little that life was good and right as it stood and that rushing ahead too fast could spoil things.

Mama made it very clear to Phoebe after Mary's party that Phoebe was not to expect to run around with Bill with any great frequency. Phoebe didn't mind; she had discovered something about Bill. She could, in his absence, invest him with fascinating qualities which had all the semblance of reality so long as Bill stayed absent. Idealized, he behaved in Phoebe's reveries in precisely the manner she desired in him. Vicariously, she found in Bill the perfection she was ever searching for in the real Bill.

In the flesh, Bill was imperfect, and Phoebe knew it well enough. Therefore, she was willing to keep him far enough in the distance to haze over any lacks she did not wish to recognize. This remote Phoebe was very puzzling to the matter of fact Bill. Overgrown and inarticulate himself, he liked Phoebe for her smallness and devastating ability to slay the unwary with verbal thrusts; and he wanted to be with her. He felt her withdrawal and, naturally, pursued her all the faster because he did not understand what he was seeking. Phoebe, on the other hand, understood Bill thoroughly and found him compassionate, dependable, someone to parade before the other girls. She was content to be his girl. But since he had kissed her at the party, Phoebe knew well enough that Bill was wonderful only when she clothed him with her sense of wonder. So she walked to and from school with him, exchanged notes and confidences, and accepted all the small gifts he offered as her rightful possession.

One Saturday, Bill startled Phoebe by arriving at her front porch in a beautiful uniform. Helen, romping about the yard, for one moment was struck dumb by the gorgeous vision. Then she was rushing down the steps the better to observe the resplendent Bill, self-consciously holding up his bicycle. Yes, it was a new uniform. In fact, Bill informed the dazzled ladies it was a new job, telegraph messenger, for after school hours and Saturdays, and would Phoebe go to church with him tomorrow night? He'd wait while she asked her mother.

Phoebe looked very hard at Bill in his beautiful uniform. She felt strange: here was Bill, just the same Bill she went to school with every day. Yet here he stood, changed, resplendent, the Bill she had been creating for herself. Was it the uniform? Phoebe began analyzing the situation minutely. Why did Bill seem so different? What made that confident look in his eyes? She felt confused, unsure of herself, who had previously been so sure.

"I don't think she'll let me, Bill," she began, then reversed herself briskly. "Wait, Bill! I'll see; I'll be right back."

Phoebe advanced upon Mama with determination and guile. Mama must let me go. She was...her thoughts trailed off. She must find out again. She must know why she suddenly wanted so badly to find out.

Mama surprised her with an easy surrender. Phoebe, primed for a battle, felt a little foolish to have won permission so easily. After she told Bill the news, his only response was his confident smile and a brief goodbye. She watched Bill ride away; she felt the old breathless expectation, the inevitable urge to explore and eventually find.

Phoebe's preparations for church held all the solemnity of a rite. She kept herself amazingly good all day Sunday: she was up on time, helped with breakfast and the household chores afterward, gave a critical eye to Helen's Sunday School preparations, and was meticulous with her own. Bill, as usual, was at Sunday School. Phoebe gave him one swift glance, no more, and hurried home with Helen. She was holding fast to a dream for the rest of the day. Perhaps if she could believe it strongly enough, she would find that Bill would fulfill her dreams even beyond her imagination.

In the afternoon, she took a book upstairs and lay on her bed to read. She remembered the few times in her life when she had held joy and fulfillment in her hand. Why must possession always, or almost always, fall so far short of pursuit? Phoebe struggled to lay hold of an evasive truth. If I am never to catch up with what I'm running after, she mused darkly, why do I run?

Mary isn't so silly. She thinks things are good enough as they are and isn't forever dashing around corners just because she hopes to find something beautiful there. I know that almost always, there will be nothing there. The sensible thing to do is to stop looking. Bill is all right, just as he is. Ah, but last night, she recalled, in his new uniform, there was something different. It had called to her clearly from the light in his eye, from the curve of his lip, from the poise of his body as he stood holding his bicycle. Phoebe dressed for church very slowly, often looking with her own eyes in her mirror. She thought wistfully of Helen's curls and Mary's wide blue eyes. Still, she wouldn't have changed herself. I'd be someone else, then, she thought, twisting her head to see the set of her wide hair ribbon.

Phoebe pulled her puffed sleeves to a jauntier angle and settled her dress about her slim waist. She tried to see all of herself at once in the mirror and admired her new patent leather slippers. She smiled to herself when she heard Mama peremptorily order Helen back downstairs after an attempted bolt to Phoebe's room. Since the slapping episode, though, Mama had been severe with Phoebe. Helen had been required to restrain herself from excessive teasing. Papa had been responsible for the new order, and he had been unexpectedly firm with Helen.

Strange that Papa, rather than Mama, should have understood Phoebe's needs. Phoebe could hear Bill downstairs, so she got into her best tan coat and the white leghorn hat with pink rosebuds. Her gloves were white silk and smelled of lavender as she pulled them on. She looked again into the brown eyes in the mirror, sighed a little at her limitations, and went downstairs.

Bill had been just Bill, after all. But he had been very winsome, pleased on the way to church. Phoebe didn't find him a Prince Charming: and neither was she disappointed. Being with Bill, she discovered, invariably brought her to earth, for Bill wasn't bothered with vain flights of imagination.

"He likes me," she thought contritely, "just as I am."

Nevertheless, if Phoebe could have changed Bill, she would have made him over thoroughly. Still, she felt they two gave a good account of themselves among the other boys and girls. She felt no embarrassment since their presence together was taken for granted. They listened gravely to the sermon, shared a songbook, and felt rather pleased with themselves.

On the way home, a loose plank in the sidewalk was Phoebe's undoing. She stumbled, clutched at Bill, and fell hard on her knees. In the half-dark, she held her breath while she endured the pain and felt Bill groping to pick her up. His hands were awkward and kind. He made a concerned and pitying sound deep in his throat, and Phoebe gave way to a flood of anguished tears.

"Oh, Bill, Bill, it hurts!" she sobbed. Bill did all the things the Bills of the world do for those they love. He cradled her in his arms, and he patted her back. She dried her tears on Bill's best handkerchief, and Bill supported her the five remaining blocks home into the heart of her concerned family, where her tortured knees received first aid and her injured pride was soothed.

Chapter 16 – Professor Johnny Smith

Left, left, left, right, left. The marching feet were Phoebe's, and they were carrying her to high school. She was putting one before the other, precisely, determinedly. Her shoulders were held high and too far back, and her exaggerated posture made her backache. But she wouldn't let down because she was correcting a bad case of rounded shoulders, and every morning she put herself through this rigid discipline.

Her ankles and knees bumped sharply together occasionally, and that was another discomfort. Phoebe had thrown away her pillow and endured Spartan nights sleeping on the front sides of her shoulders, thus pushing them farther in the direction Phoebe desired them to grow. Each night she examined herself critically, with the aid of a hand mirror, before her dresser mirror, and she knew she was becoming straighter. It never occurred to her that she might have accomplished the desired result less strenuously. Phoebe often did things the hard way.

This morning she was thinking of Professor Johnny Smith, her physical geography teacher. He taught at the nearby university and was well-versed in his travels, offering his part-time services as a high school teacher when the school needed one. Phoebe closed her eyes and marched painfully on a few steps. She was seeing Professor Smith as he greeted his first-year classes; his boyish, half-shy smile, his black alert eyes, his efficiency.

Phoebe stubbed her toe, hopped off balance in agony, and recovered herself. Left, right, left, right, left. Yesterday the Professor had smiled at her with the highest praise when she named all the counties of Oregon without a mistake. She could see that smile now: it was a wide, tender, generous smile, and it said to Phoebe whatever she wanted it to say. The words he spoke in praise, "That was excellent, Miss Miller," were nothing, empty, meaningless. But Professor Smith's smile was manna, miraculous food for Phoebe's wistful hunger. Her lips curved in unconscious imitation of the beloved smile. Like half the girls in the physical geography class, Phoebe adored her teacher.

Suddenly Phoebe thought of Bill. She felt her cheeks grow red with shame for Bill's unanswered letter. Bill had moved with his family to Colorado, and Phoebe had felt very important for a while, getting Bill's letters across the intervening miles and answering them at length with accounts of high school. Bill was going to high school, too; he found the going, as in grade school days, rough going. His letters were like himself: faithful, sturdy, unimaginative, a bit homesick, and wistful sounding. Phoebe's interest in Bill dwindled, faded, and was soon gone.

"I still like Bill," she muttered, her back a blazing ache as she made the last block and mounted the high school steps.

High school became a routine for Phoebe. English classes were fun. She liked to write, produced essays that won top grades from her English instructor, and loved the classics, particularly Shakespeare. Merchant of Venice, Hamlet, and Macbeth, she knew almost line for line, found a glow of deepest delight in a genius capable of arousing in her such profound admiration. German was next best. It was easy; it was magic: she launched into a new world with all the delight of adventure. At the beginning of her third year, Phoebe and five other faithful friends begged for another year of German beyond the two offered. A few recruits gathered to augment the original six, and the school granted the request. The small eager group was ready for adventure. Reading rapidly, its members skimmed the cream from the less complicated classics and carried their zest into the fourth year, which proved no less satisfying.

"Sometimes I dream in German," Phoebe confided this last year to her teacher.

"Phoebe," sighed gray-eyed Miss Sampson. "How I love to teach fourth-year German!"

But Phoebe's light shone only in small and friendly class groups. The school was comparatively large for Oregon and was dominated, at least socially, by a group of students representing the wealth and social position of the town. In this group Phoebe and her like had no part, nor expected to have any. Phoebe never learned to dance, partly because she was associated with boys and girls who did not dance but mostly because her evenings were given over to reading, for Phoebe still read voraciously, sometimes unwisely, whatever came her way. The round shoulders had resulted from this constant bending over a book. Reading still instantly transported Phoebe into her private world of enchantment.

Her secret adoration for Professor Johnny Smith possessed her utterly. She suffered fiercely when his friendly smile was given to other doting freshman girls but lifted no finger to keep it for herself. Not for worlds would Phoebe have had him see this hopeless, blighting emotion that held her captive. At times she hugged it to herself, sank into its waves, and was engulfed. Again she fought it with desperation, seeing it for the poor thing it was, half amused and wholly vexed at herself. For Phoebe had a certain wisdom in these matters. Adolescence sometimes exalted and crushed her spirit, but at recurrent intervals, she knew its rhythms would bring her back to sanity. So Phoebe was happier than some of her fellow sufferers, likewise worshippers at the Smith shrine, who were certain they should die of their disease.

Today Phoebe finished her algebra for tomorrow, gathered her physical geography text and her newly finished contour map, and sat waiting for the bell.

Chapter 16

"In just a few minutes, I'll see him again. Phoebe mused, "For a whole class period, I can see him and listen to his voice. She glanced across the aisle at Mary. Mary was daydreaming, her blue eyes gazing vacantly out the window. She was twisting the long-suffering curl above her left ear. She was wrapped in secret thought, her lips curved to a goofy smile. Mary was openly infatuated with Professor Smith. Suddenly Phoebe's face blazed with furious self-contempt. That is precisely how I look most of the time; she raged at herself—like a moon-faced calf.

The bell rang jarringly, and Phoebe leaped into the aisle and rushed for the classroom. Something was breaking up within her, and she felt bludgeoned by contending forces. Simultaneously, her mind ran swiftly beside her tumultuous emotions, for Phoebe must ever analyze and probe herself. Her swift dash brought her early to the class, and she dropped into a back-row chair—a bird's eye view of the situation suited Phoebe best today. The room filled rapidly with laughter, students talking and slamming books. Then Professor Johnny Smith walked in, smiled compellingly, and efficiently took over the class.

Phoebe's eyes had lost their raptness and look of trance. They were challenging and critical, taking in every feature and each intonation. Almost at once, Phoebe felt a release, an escape. She felt her ridiculous shackles falling away. Phoebe, in the twinkling of an eye, clothed herself in pride and self-righteousness. Professor Smith's bright black eyes found Phoebe and questioned her expertly concerning Oregon's prehistoric coastline. Phoebe knew the answer; she tossed it back to him with smiling malice. She had escaped the bondage of unrequited love. She was free again.

Chapter 17 – Timid William

Helen was growing up. Her cheeks were as red, her eyes as sparkling as ever, but her little girl traits were merging into early adolescence. She had a forthright dominance that made all her paths shortcuts to her desires' fulfillment. Without being ruthless, Helen took what she wanted from life. She was not tortured, as was Phoebe, by attacks of conscience, indecision, and feelings of futility. Helen believed in herself, knew what she wanted, and went for it directly. This sense of direction and goal orientation that was Helen's was not for Phoebe, who must feel her way, test her footing, and endlessly search her heart. Phoebe behaved as if her ideals might momentarily desert her and change overnight into something foreign to her personality. She recognized these moments of departure from her character and tolerated them. At the same time, she accepted them as part of herself, which she could not disown. Phoebe would not have traded lives with anyone, although she was far from satisfied with herself. Phoebe secretly conceded that Helen's ways were simpler, more direct, and possibly even more honest.

Helen was as large as Phoebe, despite the six years difference in their ages, a distinction that tended to seem less as time advanced. Helen was already putting away her dolls. Indeed she had never really loved them. Phoebe still cherished several dolls in a drawer of the bureau. Only to the casual eye had she put away these childish things. In reality, she had never given them up, for to do so would have seemed to cripple herself, so much a part of her had these symbols of her happy childhood become. Occasionally, behind her locked door, she took out the birthday doll, sat on her bed, and cradled its stiff body in her arms. Such moments frightened Phoebe, for they were poignant with both pain and pleasure, so delicately balanced that the least disturbing of the scales threatened her peace of mind. Trembling at such times, Phoebe would observe herself almost as a split personality. On one side was the shadowy presence of herself at four years old, sitting in a little rocker and holding both a doll and unbearable happiness in her arms. But side-by-side with this image, there was always another of herself caressing a living child, her firstborn.

Papa and Mama were taking a more leisurely pace in their later years. Life was less strenuous in town, and the small feed mill business, prospering for several years, was still thriving. But Mama wanted a new home, all the plans on paper, and a building site in mind. Papa was tolerant of Mama's ambitions and not averse to the new house, though he was content enough with the comfortable one to which he had become accustomed. Phoebe and Helen used all their persuasive powers with Papa for the new house. It would mean a lovely room for each and ample closet space. And electricity! And a furnace! Before their ardent hopes, Papa's last defenses were down, and soon the initial plans were perfected, and the actual construction began.

William was six years old. He was tiny indeed and very timid. When other more exuberant children played noisily, he watched from a discreet distance, smiling wistfully at the fun, edging vigorously nearer, or retreating abruptly as his daring diminished. Any attempts on the part of his family to make him an active role in such groups failed. He was still too fearful of life to venture further than to its fringe.

With Phoebe, Will would go anywhere, his small hand closely clasped in hers. Phoebe understood his nameless fears and defended them fiercely from Helen's impatience.

"He can't be a baby all his life," Helen would argue. "What will he do when he has to go to school?"

Helen would bend her dark brows severely upon the shrinking William, and his terrified eyes would look desperately into Phoebe's. Oh, yes, Phoebe understood so well! She remembered from years past her little fearful cry. "I won't go to school! I'll never go to school!" She took William on her lap and told him, with grown-up chuckles, of Phoebe, who wouldn't go to school.

"It will be fun, William, she promised. "One day, you'll be afraid to go, and then it will be tomorrow, and you'll be there, and when you come home, you'll say, "Why was I ever afraid of school? Because it's fun!"

William drew a long breath, a hardly convinced breath.

"Will I, Phoebe?" he whispered, "Will I?"

Chapter 18 - Richard

One evening, as Phoebe was finishing tomorrow's assignment of "William Tell," Mary burst in.

"He's coming! Richard! He's coming next week."

Phoebe promptly abandoned "William Tell."

"Mary! What is he like? Will he live here?"

Richard was Mary's cousin, a son of Mary's mother's sister, long expected and eagerly awaited. Mary had a small photograph of Richard, which Phoebe had seen. Phoebe was almost as excited as Mary.

Papa began teasing, "Tom, Dick, or Harry, which ones will they marry?" This continued until Phoebe and Mary, giggling and with Helen in tow, fled to Phoebe's room. They threw themselves across Phoebe's big bed and speculated at length on the imminent Richard.

"Of course," sighed Mary, "He's terribly old, twenty-six at least, but you'll like him, Phoebe, you'll love him! When Mama and I visited his home two years ago, he took me everyplace, and we had fun!"

Mary wiggled rapturously, Phoebe's eyes sparkled, but ten-year-old Helen slid off the bed in disgust

"Twenty-six years old!" she flung back from the stairway. "Why, the man's old enough to be both your fathers!"

At Mary's and Phoebe's derisive shout, Helen slammed the stair door. The two lay looking at each other, sharing this shiny new expectation. They were smiling identically, dreamily speculatively. Then Mary murmured, "of course, he's old enough to be both our fathers," and both girls rolled on Phoebe's bed and pealed their laughter through the house.

And that was the last glimpse Eunice gave us of her life as Phoebe, but we can hope we uncover more somewhere! She did choose to leave

us the following poem, which adeptly reminds us of how fleeting life can be, but how God holds it all.

I

One's soul grows full by spending;
The world's an empty cup
Until one's drinking from it
Fills it up.

II

A lovely thing is dignity
To move among no matter what fine farms of sod
With this significant equality:
That I, too, have my being straight from God.

III

Fields behind the houses
Aren't far,
And the fields are open to
Sun, moon, star:
Come out—beyond your clutterings
You are

IV

In the room, my watch ticked;
Outside against a tree
The moon wove time from branch to branch
More leisurely

Phoebe

V

God in eternity throws away time,
He doesn't worry when I squander mine:
"Here's a new day to spend; here's a new year—
You've lost them!
Well, here's a new moment, my dear."

Elsie McDowall

Epilogue

And time did fly, just as the poem that Phoebe left for us says. Phoebe never did publish her book, but God knew her great-grandaughter would find it and enjoy it and publish it one day!

And so, just as my ancestor and Great Great Great Great Grandfather, Dr. Moors Farwell, is remembered "for his life of faith and good works," which "is known and read by all men, and by this, he being dead yet speaketh," so too now may Phoebe's life be memorialized, including Dr. Moors Farwell's impact on it. We know from Phoebe's own words that she did "bargain" with God and was, in her immature state at that time, unsure of her status with the Almighty. However, I believe her family would have attested that she did not stay immature in her faith but did, in her unique way, become reconciled and at peace with Him in the end.

Phoebe knew the importance of waiting for the right time for love, for "she did realize a little that life was good and right as it stood and that rushing ahead too fast could spoil things." How fortunate that is! Although Bill was a lovely gentleman, he did not possess all the qualities Phoebe sought in a man. Neither did her childhood crush, Henry, nor Professor Johnny Smith. Mary's cousin, Richard, wasn't the one either. However, there was later the incomparable "Tom."

Phoebe mentioned Tom at the start of her story, and he was the one worth waiting for in the end. "Oh, God, let there always be Tom! Let the children come and go, if must be, let them even stay away, but let there always be Tom coming home to me from work at night. Tom, with his unruffled patience, his unfailing fairness, his need of me, his maddening obstinancy, his more than human charity for human frailty. Ah, Tom!"

Tom's name in real life was Harvey Elmer Tobie. He possessed the intellect and other outstanding qualities mentioned above that Phoebe was looking for in a man. He earned his Ph.D. and wrote books of his own.

If "Tom" and "Phoebe" had never found each other, there would have been no Daniela Robins and, indeed, no Robins Wings Publishing Company!

Robins Wings Publishing Company exists to let the world know about the love of God and his faithfulness. We do not need to bargain with God as Phoebe did since works do not save us but only by God's grace are we saved, and the works that stem from that are the fruit of that gift.